FOWL PLAY

DEWBERRY FARM MYSTERIES

KAREN MACINERNEY

For Chris, with all my love.

This book is a work of fiction. Names, characters, places, and incidents are either products of the author's imagination or used fictitiously. Any resemblance to actual events or locales or persons, living or dead, is entirely coincidental.

Books in the Dewberry Farm Mystery Series

Killer Jam

Fatal Frost

Deadly Brew

Mistletoe Murder

Dyeing Season

Wicked Harvest

Sweet Revenge

Peach Clobber

 Created with Vellum

1

September in Texas is not the most glamorous month. After the punishing heat of June, July, and August, I always feel entitled to the northern winds sweeping through and blowing all that hot air out to sea, at least for a day or two, so that I don't spend half my waking hours trying to give my veggies and fruit trees enough water to keep them alive. Our other source of relief, much to the consternation of our southeastern neighbors on the Gulf coast, is often a good hurricane or tropical depression that refills the stock ponds and provides the parched, cracking soil much-needed moisture. You could almost hear the earth sigh in relief when the rains of fall arrived, and the fresh, earthy smell of those first drops on heat-baked soil is one of my favorite things.

Now, though, as I surveyed the sun-bleached pasture outside my little yellow farmhouse, I felt a sense of foreboding. We'd been deluged with rain until July, but hadn't seen a drop in almost six weeks... including all of August, which usually brought at least a little rain from disturbances in the Gulf of Mexico.

This September had been worse than usual, unfortunately. Despite a gift of early summer rains (too much, in fact—there had been flooding), we'd had a dry winter and spring, and were still behind on rainfall for the year. Wells were starting to run dry all over the county, and I was having to bring in expensive hay for my little herd of goats and cows... and make tough decisions about which crops to keep alive and which ones to let go. Every day the water stream from my well became more of a trickle, and I was worried that one day soon there would be nothing to pump. The well level was occupying my mind more and more as the heat kept coming.

I wasn't the only one suffering, but it wasn't much comfort. All the ranchers and farmers in Buttercup spent more time than we'd like to admit studying weather forecasts and hoping to see the temperature dip somewhere below three digits and the rain chances to go above 0%, but so far, it was midway through the month and there was no relief in sight. Already a few of the ranchers were making noises about selling up to city folks looking to buy a weekend property... and the last thing I wanted to do after spending the past several years building up the farm I'd spent childhood summers on was give up everything I'd built and move back to Houston.

Sadly, despite being just days from the autumnal equinox, the only sign of impending fall on the farm was the pumpkin spice muffins my best friend Quinn had started making at the Blue Onion cafe. I was in the mood to turn the oven on, whip up a batch of my own favorite pumpkin bread (I had a couple dozen sugar pumpkins survive both the flooding and the late summer drought, and a few of them were ripe), and turn my already struggling air conditioner down far enough so that I could pretend it was fall.

My desire to be able to pay my electric bill was stronger, though, so I limited myself to washing down a crunchy, streusel-laden bite of Quinn's muffin with a tall glass of iced tea I'd garnished with a sprig of the spearmint I'd planted under the faucet on the side of the house.

My rescue poodle Chuck whined at me from where he was splayed out under the air conditioning, and I tossed him a chunk of muffin, which he gulped down immediately. Tobias, Chuck's vet and my boyfriend, wouldn't approve, but Chuck and I had an unspoken agreement not to tell him. My well-padded poodle swallowed the muffin chunk, looked at me hopefully for a moment, and then dropped his head down on the floor again, apparently exhausted from the effort. I'd shaved the poor thing down until he was almost bald, but it was still too hot for him.

Smoky and Lucky, the two kittens I had rescued from the chimney of the smokehouse a while back, were the only farmhouse residents unfazed by the heat; while Chuck and I sweated, they frolicked in a sunbeam, chasing one of the catnip mice I'd picked up for them the other day.

I had finished the last of my tea and was contemplating pouring myself another when the phone rang. I picked it up; it was Quinn.

"Hey, you," I said. "I'm just finishing that pumpkin spice muffin you gave me yesterday."

"They're good, aren't they?" she asked. "I added extra pecans and brown sugar streusel to the top this time, and layered some in the middle, too, kind of like a sour cream coffee cake."

"It's working for me," I said. "They're amazing, and I love the bit of vanilla glaze, too. You should seriously enter them into a cooking contest."

"You know, I hadn't thought about that," she said. "That

might be good for business. But would somebody steal the recipe?"

"Absolutely they would," I said. "But since you're the only bakery in Buttercup, I wouldn't worry about that too much. Besides, your maple twists are already known in three counties."

"Only three?" she asked, and I could hear the smile in her voice. "Anyway, the reason I called is that I want your advice on something."

I sat up a little straighter. "Is Jed back on the streets again?" Jed, Quinn's violent ex, had stalked my friend several times in the past; he'd even come out to Dewberry Farm one night when she was staying with me. I would never forget how he'd kicked poor Chuck into a wall that night... or how things might have been different if he'd been carrying one of his guns.

"No," she said. "He's not up for parole for another few months at least, thank goodness. I was actually calling to talk about Peter."

That was a relief; I liked Peter, an amazing farmer who ran an organic farm called Green Haven here in Buttercup. Not only had he taught me all about raising goats and given me my starter herd, but he was so dedicated to earth-friendly practices that he drove a fry-oil-powered bus to the farmers' markets in Austin on weekends. Peter and Quinn had been seeing each other for some time, and I had loved watching my friend blossom in the relationship. Her laugh had become easier and she smiled quickly now, the wariness I knew from when we'd first met slowly melting away. I hoped things were still good between them.

"You guys doing okay?" I asked, feeling a twinge of worry.

"We are," she confirmed. "In fact... I was thinking of moving in with him, and I wanted to ask your advice."

"Wow," I said. "That's a big step. I didn't know you guys were talking about it."

"We weren't," she said. "Or at least I wasn't. But I was out there with Pip this past weekend, and he seemed so much happier having room to run in the yard, the idea just kind of came up. At my place, I always have to put Pip on a leash and walk him around the square... it's hard on a big, young dog."

Pip was Quinn's big lab-mix, who was still young; we'd found him abandoned a few years back and he and Quinn had bonded immediately. She had given him a great life, but she was right; her little apartment above the Blue Onion didn't give him a lot of room to roam. Still, I wasn't sure more roaming room for Pip was the best motivation to move in with Peter.

"Is Pip the only reason?" I asked, looking out at the sun-bleached pasture where Blossom, my escape-artist cow, was currently sheltering in the shadow of the barn. She looked a little listless in the heat. I needed to buy more hay for everyone, I thought, feeling another familiar twinge of anxiety at the expense of keeping everyone fed... and watered.

"Of course Pip isn't the only reason I'm moving in," Quinn said, snapping me back from my worries. "My landlord raised the rent a ton, so it's also a cost-saving measure. Also, I just... I don't know. It feels like it's time."

"What does that mean?" I asked.

"I guess I've always pictured myself married, with kids. I'm not getting any younger. And if Peter and I are going to make a go of it..."

"You want to do a trial run?" I finished for her.

"Yeah," she said. "If it's not going to work, I kind of want to know sooner than later."

"That makes sense," I said.

"Still, I'm annoyed with my landlord. The rent went way up for both the cafe and my apartment."

"Those pesky landlords," I said.

"How's your AirBnB going, anyway?"

"So far, so good," I said, glancing out the window at the little wood house down by the creek. The Buttercup German Club had helped me move the historic building to the site a while back and even assisted me with some of the renovations, and now I rented it out short-term to help pay the farm's bills. "I've got another tenant moving in later on today, as it turns out. She'll be here for at least a month."

"That's a long time. What's she here for?"

"She says she's researching the area for investment purposes. Her name is Jo Nesbit, but I didn't get a chance to talk to her. All we really did is set up the rental; I'll find out more when she gets here."

"I hope she's nice."

"Me too," I said. "If not, at least she paid up front. When are you planning to move, by the way?"

"This weekend," she said.

"Wow. Need help?"

"Only if you have time," she said.

"I always have time for you," I told her, and hung up a moment later, feeling oddly disturbed by our conversation. My friend was moving in with her boyfriend. Why should that bother me?

I was still thinking about that as I grabbed my egg basket and headed out to check on the girls. After milking everyone and watering that morning, I hadn't gotten around to checking the nest boxes; instead, I'd come in and taken an accidental nap on the couch.

As I walked out to the coop, something seemed... wrong. Instead of the normal clucking and scratching noises, all I heard was the hot breeze soughing through the tall, dry stalks of the native grassland patch behind the fence. When I got to the coop, I realized what was wrong.

The coop door was open.

And all of my girls were gone.

2

"Hester! Niblet!" I called, looking wildly around for any sign of my little flock. They'd gotten out before when I hadn't latched the door correctly, but a few chickens always stayed inside, and the rest never strayed far. Had they gone down to the trees on Dewberry Creek to get out of the heat?

I hurried down to the creek, scanning the trees for signs of my feathered menagerie, but the creek was as quiet as the coop had been, without even a trickle of water to interrupt the sound of the wind.

Where had they gone?

I searched the farm methodically, walking up and down the dewberry bushes along the creek calling for them, winding through my small peach orchard, checking the fields to make sure they hadn't decided to make lunch of my few pumpkins, and even poking my head into the barn and the outbuildings.

There was no sign of my chickens anywhere.

I called Tobias as I walked back to the coop, still searching for any hint of what might have happened to my flock. When I poked my head inside, I found one lonely chicken—Penny—tucked up in the darkest nesting box and making small, worried clucks.

"What happened to everyone?" I asked Penny as Tobias's phone rang. I was petting her head to soothe her (she had no answer for me) when my boyfriend answered.

"What's up?" he asked.

"The chickens are gone."

"Oh, no. Did we leave the coop door open?"

"It was open," I said, "but they seem to have—literally—flown the coop."

"They're not in the fields?"

"Or the barn, or the trees by the creek, or anywhere I can see," I told him.

"I guess there is a chicken rustler in town, then," he said.

"A chicken rustler?" I asked, still stroking Penny.

"One of the ranchers whose cows I was checking out the other day said he was hit just last week. Lost about fifteen hens. Apparently he's not the only one."

"Why would anyone steal chickens?"

"Your guess is as good as mine," he said. "You should report it to the police."

"For all the good that will do," I said. Our local sheriff was not what you'd call the best and brightest. "I'm worried about them, though. At least they left Penny behind... but she looks scared to death."

"Chickens are flock animals," he said. "I'll bet she's scared."

I sighed. "I can't take her into the house because of the cats."

"Hopefully we'll find everyone else and she'll have her buddies back soon," he said.

"I'm not counting on it," I said, "but I appreciate your

optimism." My heart sank as I hung up and dialed the local police station, Penny's sad clucking continuing. Opal Gruber answered, to my relief; I liked Opal. She kept a ready supply of Southern Livings and Texas Monthlys in the station jail cell—not that I'd had to avail myself of them, at least not to date—and had been a help to me on on multiple occasions when our bumbling sheriff, Rooster Kocurek, was worse than useless.

"Opal!" I said. "It's Lucy Resnick."

"Lucy! How are you?"

"I've been better," I admitted, and told her about the chickennapping.

"Well, dagnabbit! That's the fourth time this week," she told me.

"Tobias told me I wasn't the only one," I said.

"When did it happen?"

"Sometime between last night and this morning. I was late getting out to check on them today, so I can't give you a better estimate, I'm afraid."

"Probably last night then," she said. "That's when the rest of 'em have happened... after dark. Chuck make any noise during the wee hours?"

"I actually wasn't home last night," I said. I'd spent the night at Tobias's house, a few blocks off the square.

"Uh huh," she said. "If I had a boyfriend as cute as yours, I wouldn't be stayin' home most nights either," she said, and I felt myself blush. "I hear Peter and Quinn are lookin' to move in together, speakin' of cute boyfriends. Now that man is a tall, cool drink of water... not that yours isn't, mind you."

"Yeah, she told me today," I said.

"Too bad about Gus and Flora, though."

I blinked. "What?"

"I ran into Fannie down at Fannie's Antiques during my

lunch break. Fannie called me and said she had a pie safe that would be just perfect for the station kitchen, and I thought I'd snatch it up before one of the tourists nabbed it. Anyway, Flora was there at the jewelry counter, eyes all puffed up and swollen, and told me she and Gus called it quits just this week."

"I don't believe it. They just announced a date for the wedding!" Gus Holz and Flora Kocurek had met a few years back; Gus had been a confirmed bachelor for decades, and Flora had just come out from years under her mother's thumb... and a bad relationship with a man who planned to marry her for her money and then get rid of Flora so he could inherit her estate. Flora and Gus had been deliriously in love for quite some time now, and they'd both been glowing when they announced their engagement just a month or two back. "What happened?"

"I think you'd have to ask Flora that," Opal said. "She wasn't in a particularly conversational mood. In fact, she was looking to sell her engagement ring."

"Sell her engagement ring? But she's got so much money... why would she do that?"

"She said she couldn't stand looking at it, or even having it in the house."

"I'll talk to her and find out what happened. Maybe it's fixable."

"I think that horse is out of the barn and halfway to Fort Worth by now, but no harm in tryin', I suppose," Opal said mournfully. "But you didn't call to talk about Gus and Flora. Let me get one of the deputies to come out and take a look and you can fill out an incident report. Are you around later this morning?"

"I am," I said.

"I'll send someone out as soon as I can rustle one of 'em

up on the radio," she said. "I hope you find your girls. And let me know what you find out about Gus and Flora! I was goin' to go dress shoppin' this weekend, but if the weddin's off..."

"Don't change your plans yet," I said. "It may be salvageable. I'll let you know as soon as I find out what's up."

I got off the phone and left a message for Quinn, wondering if she had any news, and then called Flora. The call went directly to voicemail. "This is Flora Kocurek. I can't come to the phone right now, but please leave a message. Unless this is Gus, in which case don't bother. If you're not Gus, I'll try and get back to you as soon as I can."

I groaned and left a message asking her to call me back pronto. As much as I hated to admit it, I thought as I hung up, it sounded like Opal might have been right.

DEPUTY FARNON ARRIVED about an hour after I discovered the chickens missing. He was a young man, barely out of high school, with the gangly look of a boy who'd sprouted up so fast he hadn't yet caught up with himself. "Where's the coop, ma'am?" he asked after accepting my offer of an iced tea.

"Out back," I said. He drained his glass and set it on the table on the front porch, then followed me back to where the chickens had lived until earlier that morning. I'd done another sweep of the farm and turned up no sign of them, although I spotted a few boot prints I didn't recognize in the dust beside the gravel driveway.

The sun was high in the sky, and the hot breeze made me feel like I was walking through a giant convection oven as we neared the chicken yard, which seemed forlorn without its normal residents pecking for bugs in the dirt. I lifted the latch of the coop door.

"You keep this locked?" the young deputy asked.

"I didn't," I said as we stepped inside. The darkness of the coop was a welcome relief after the searing brightness outside. "But I might going forward."

"How many are missin'?" he asked, poking around the coop nervously, as if the chickennapper might still be lurking in the shadows somewhere.

"Twenty-four," I said. "They missed the last one; she's in the corner over there," I said, pointing out Penny, who was still clucking worriedly in her nest box. "Opal mentioned there's been a rash of chicken thefts. Who else has been hit?"

"The Krugers, the Slovaceks, and the Muellers," he said. "All in the past week. Never seen anythin' like it in Buttercup. Sheriff hasn't, either."

"Any leads?"

He shook his head. "No, ma'am. Leastwise not so far."

"I found a boot print I don't recognize," I said. When he was done looking for the missing chickens, or evidence, or whatever he was searching for, we stepped out of the coop. I latched it behind me, feeling the sun blast down again, and led him to the place in the driveway.

"It's right here," I said, pointing at the print in the gravel. There was no tread, but you could see the length of it; it looked as if whoever it was had swiveled, maybe as he was getting into a car.

"You sure?" he asked, peering down at the print.

I nodded. "Too big to be mine. It looks like a man's boot print to me, and it's not my boyfriend's." I waited a moment, but he looked unsure as to how he should proceed. "I took a picture of it," I prompted, "but I was thinking it might not be a bad idea to measure it."

He gave me a look that suggested my input was not entirely welcome. "Could be anyone. I imagine lots of folks in and out of here."

"Not really," I said.

"All right," he said. "I'll measure it. Probably won't come to anythin', but you never know."

"Do you need a tape measure?"

"That would be mighty helpful," he said. As I walked back to the farmhouse to grab one, Tobias's truck rolled up the driveway. I waved as he parked next to my little truck.

"I'm just running in to get a tape measure," I said. "We've got a boot print that might belong to the chickennapper."

"I've got a tape measure in my truck," he said.

"Howdy, Dr. Brandt," the deputy said, hailing him from beside the suspect boot print.

"Hi, Bart," Tobias said, reaching over to the glove box to get a tape measure. "Any idea who the chicken rustler is yet?"

"No, sir. We're on the case, though."

"Good," Tobias said as the young man took a picture of the print with his own phone, then laid the tape measure out next to it and took another. Which was actually good thinking, surprisingly.

"Well, I'm headin' back into town now," Deputy Farnon said. "If anythin' else comes up, you let me know, okay?" He reached into his pocket and pulled out a dog-eared business card, handing it to me.

"Thanks," I said, taking the card and tucking it into the pocket of my shorts. "Keep us posted."

"We will, ma'am," he said. Then he tipped an imaginary hat and strode back to his truck. He reminded me of a teenage boy in a Halloween costume, pretending to be a cop.

As he backed up and turned down the driveway, I sighed. "I'm afraid I'll never see my girls again."

"You never know," Tobias said, leaning over to give me a kiss. "Don't give up hope."

"Want a glass of iced tea?" I asked. "And maybe a sandwich?"

"Actually, I thought I might take you out to lunch, if you've got time."

"I've always got time for you," I said.

"Rosita's?" he asked.

"I could go for a good plate of enchiladas," I said. "I'm in!"

3

Rosita's, Buttercup's fabled Mexican restaurant, was busy as always at lunch; we were lucky there were any tables at all.

Marcy Koch, one of the servers, greeted us. "Two for lunch?" she asked.

"Yes, please," Tobias said.

"I've got just the spot." She grabbed two menus and led us to a booth near the front door, then brought over a basket of fresh tortilla chips and salsa.

"These are my weakness," I said as I dipped one of the warm, salty chips in the bowl of fresh salsa, which was made with fire-roasted tomatoes and jalapeños, lime, and just the right amount of onion and cilantro.

"Mine too," Tobias said, joining me. "Other than you, of course."

I smiled at him, and I was reaching for a second chip when a familiar person walked through the front door.

"It's Flora," I said. I'd filled Tobias in on what I'd found out about the broken engagement on the way to the restaurant.

Tobias glanced over at her and his eyebrows rose. "She's alone."

"No surprise, considering the circumstances. I'm going to invite her to join us, if you don't mind."

"Of course I don't mind," he said. I was already out of my booth and on my way to the entryway.

"Flora!" I said.

She turned to me; her face was more gaunt than usual, and her eyes were red.

"We were just sitting down to lunch; come join us." I took her arm gently.

"I just... are you sure?" she asked.

"Positive," I said. "Come sit down. We've got a booth right here."

Flora allowed me to lead her to our table. I waited until she'd slid into the booth across from Tobias, and then scooted in next to my honey.

"I heard the news. Are you okay?" I asked.

She nodded, jutting her sharp chin out. Then her face crumpled and she burst into tears. "No," she confessed. "No, I'm not okay."

I reached across the table and grabbed her bony hand, cradling it in mine. "What happened, Flora?"

"He... he won't move in with me!"

"Wait... what?"

"All this time I thought he'd move to my house. And now he wants us to move to a new place."

"Right," Tobias said, sliding me a glance.

"I've spent my whole life in my momma's house. I can't move!" She sniffled. "But he said we need a place that's ours as a couple's, not mine and not his, if we're going to make it together."

"I can see the wisdom in that," I said gently. "You've got a lot of history at your mother's house. Maybe it is time to step into something new, so to speak."

Flora blinked at me. "Leave my history behind? What, has Gus been talking to you behind my back?" She scooted out of the booth and stood up. "Clearly you don't understand," she said, and marched to the front of the restaurant, pushing through the front door, while I gawped after her. What had just happened?

"Well, that went well," Tobias said.

"Was I too forward?" I asked.

"I don't think so," he said. "But something's going on there besides just the house, I think."

"I think you're right. You think Flora's freaking out?"

"Well, obviously," he said. "But I have the feeling the house is just a symbol."

"Hmm. Of what, I wonder? Maybe of giving up control?"

"Flora did live under a domineering mother's thumb for half a century," he pointed out. "Maybe she's afraid that by getting married she'd be giving up some of her autonomy, which she really hasn't had for very long."

"And being forced to leave her home is a symbol of it," I suggested.

"Exactly."

I grinned and reached for another chip. "You know, if you change your mind about veterinary medicine, you would make a fine psychologist, Dr. Brandt."

He laughed, but didn't have time to respond... because we were interrupted by the loud thunk, followed by the sound of yelling from the direction of the kitchen. "Get out. Now!"

~

I SWIVELED around in my booth as a woman I'd never seen before scuttled from the kitchen, glancing over her shoulder as Rosita Vargas followed her with a cleaver raised in her right hand.

As we watched, the woman—who was wearing a pinstripe suit that must have been miserable in the 100-degree-plus weather—scuttled out the front door. The hot breeze made her stiff bob blow into her face. She pushed it back behind her ears, glancing back at the restaurant with a thin-lipped grimace, and made a beeline for a bright white Range Rover. She was already on her phone by the time she made it to the driver's door, and was in animated conversation as she pulled out of the parking lot a moment later, almost colliding with a Chevy pick-up truck.

"What was that all about?" I asked Marcy as she came back to the table to take our orders.

"New landlord coming in," she said, rolling her eyes. "That lady is their representative. She just told Rosita what the new rent is and then said she needs to spend ten thousand dollars to upgrade the kitchen."

"Ouch," I said. "Rosita didn't seem to take it very well, but I can understand why."

"Well, that lady told her if she didn't sign a new lease with the landlord's terms, there's a chain Tex-Mex restaurant from Dallas that would be happy to take the space."

"A chain restaurant? That's a horrible idea," Tobias said.

I shook my head. "No wonder things got ugly."

"Exactly," Marcy said, glancing out at where the Range Rover had recently pulled out of the parking lot. "She's lucky she got out in one piece. Rosita's not been herself lately, and now this..."

"What's been going on?" I asked.

"Ernesto's been sick," she said. "He was diagnosed with

lung cancer, and he's been back and forth to Houston for chemo and radiation for months. And even with insurance, it's still expensive... the rent hike is the last thing the family needs right now." She sighed. "I wish Mark Vogelsang's daughters hadn't sold the place to an out-of-towner when he passed. Or that the Vargases had bought the building ten years ago."

I understood what she meant. With the population boom and changing work patterns, the Buttercup area had had an influx of city folk... and the increased property values and property taxes to go with it. "Quinn Sloane's rent went way up, too."

"She owns the Blue Onion, right?" Marcy asked.

I nodded. "I'm worried for all the businesses in town; it's hard enough to be a small business owner without the tax hikes. I'm so sorry to hear Rosita and Ernesto are having troubles, though. I wish Mandy had told me what was going on with her father," I said. "I would be happy to drop off meals, help with driving... whatever they need." Mandy, the local editor of the *Buttercup Zephyr*, was Rosita and Ernesto's daughter, and a friend. I'd been a journalist once, and she'd invited me to work part-time for the paper, actually, but I hadn't taken her up on it so far.

"Ernesto is trying to keep it quiet. Doesn't want anyone to know, or treat him differently because he's sick, I guess." She glanced back toward the kitchen. "So you didn't hear it from me."

"Gotcha," I said.

"And I almost forgot to ask. Are you two ready to order?"

"We are," I said, and Tobias nodded. "Chicken chipotle enchiladas for me, please," I said. I could almost taste the smoky, spicy red sauce and the jack cheese already; I reached for another chip and chomped down. I was going to have to roll out of the restaurant at the rate I was going.

"And chiles rellenos for me, please," Tobias said.

"Beef, or cheese?"

"Beef."

"Got it," she said. She took our menus and headed back to the kitchen, and Tobias and I looked at each other.

"It won't be the same without Rosita's," Tobias said.

"We don't know that it's coming to that," I said. "Who bought the building, anyway?"

"I don't know," he said, "but that woman wasn't a local."

I sighed. "I don't like the idea of corporations or wealthy out-of-towners becoming landlords of our town institutions."

"Is that what happened to the Blue Onion, too?"

"I don't know if someone bought it or the rent just went up," I said, "but Quinn is planning to move in with Peter instead of renewing her lease."

"That'll be good for Pip, for sure," Tobias said. "Not a lot of room for a dog on the square."

"I know, but I kind of think decisions like that should be made because it feels right, not because money's tight, you know?"

"I agree," he said. "Wow. I thought spring was the time when love was supposed to be in the air, not late September. What's with all these people moving in together?"

"Or not, in the case of Gus and Flora."

"I'm still not convinced," Tobias said.

"Apparently Flora was trying to sell her engagement ring at Fannie's Antiques yesterday. And her voicemail message says anyone but Gus is welcome to leave a message."

"Okay, maybe I'm a little more convinced. Maybe we should talk to her."

"It certainly went swimmingly a moment ago. Maybe the second try will be the charm." I sighed. "Everything's going south today, isn't it?"

"If Rosita's is closing down, I'd say it's a crisis situation." We crunched our chips moodily until the food arrived on big, warm platters. I took a bite of my enchiladas and closed my eyes, savoring the smoky heat of the chipotle sauce, the tender chicken, and the melted cheese. "These enchiladas are a spiritual experience," I said. "It would be a crime to close down the restaurant."

"We should talk to Mandy," Tobias suggested. "See what she's dug up on the building's new owners."

"Because you know she has," I said. Mandy might be working at a small-town paper, but she was a top-notch reporter. She had a way of finding things out that not everyone was thrilled about... including me, a few times in the past. "I'll text her after I'm done eating. But right now? I'm going to enjoy these enchiladas."

"And me my chile relleno," Tobias said, scooping up a bit of guacamole with a bite of beef-stuffed Anaheim pepper. "You're right," he said once he'd swallowed a bite. "It's divine."

I put my worries aside for now and dug in, grateful to live in a place that had excellent Mexican food and savoring every bite. You have to grab good moments when you can... because things can turn in an instant.

As I was about to find out.

4

We were both stuffed when Tobias turned up the driveway toward Dewberry Farm.

"Someone else is here," he said, pointing to a white SUV next to the Ulrich House.

"My tenant Jo Nesbit is arriving this afternoon; looks like she may have gotten here early."

"Ummm... I think we've seen this woman before."

"It couldn't be," I said as we bumped up the drive.

"I think it is." The white SUV was a Range Rover, and sitting on the little front porch of the house was the woman we'd seen hurrying out of Rosita's less than an hour earlier, a suitcase beside her. She'd taken off her suit jacket, but her face was bright red and I could see sweat stains beginning to bloom on her silk blouse. She was still on her phone.

I groaned. "I'm going to be sleeping next to the enemy."

"Maybe you can influence her to let the Vargases stay?"

"It's worth a try," I said as he pulled into the spot next to my truck. I looked over at him. "Thanks again for lunch."

"Anytime," he said, reaching over to give my hand a

squeeze before I got out of the truck. "Let me know how it goes, okay?"

"Of course." I shut the truck door behind me and waved to the woman on the porch, who held up one finger. I pointed toward the farmhouse to indicate that that was the direction I was headed, and she nodded.

I had just pulled a pot of milk out of the fridge and was heating it on the stove to make cheese when there was a rap on the front door. I grabbed the cottage key from the hook beside the window and hurried to answer it.

"You must be Jo," I said when I opened the door to the suited woman.

"I'm a little early... I hope that's okay."

"No problem," I said. "Let me show you around."

"That won't be necessary," she said, glancing at her Apple Watch. "I've got another call in five minutes... there's a wifi password, right?"

"It's in a folder in the cottage," I said, handing her the key. "I'm around this evening if you'd like a glass of tea or wine, or even a beer."

"I'll see what the schedule looks like. Thanks," she said, as her phone started ringing again. She answered it and turned back toward the cottage, nodding at me. "Yes," she said. "I just talked with the owner. She was... unhappy. I told her she has until Friday to sign the new paperwork or we're going to proceed with the new tenant."

Her voice trailed off, and I stifled a sigh as I closed the front door. Something about the woman's voice told me my chances of dissuading her from letting Rosita's stay without a rent increase were very, very slim.

Still, I told myself, it never hurts to try.

~

SHE NEVER DID COME BACK, and I spent the afternoon whipping up a batch of fresh mozzarella cheese for the weekend market. By the time I'd done the chores, had supper, and was ready for bed, I had a good amount of stock waiting in the fridge. I went out to the chicken coop to check on poor lonely little Penny one more time, and then snuggled up in bed with Chuck and the cats in the bedroom that had been mine when I was a child. I still felt my grandmother's presence from time to time, often accompanied by a whiff of her lavender scent. It had been a while since I'd smelled it, and as I lay back on my pillow, my fingers playing in the soft fur behind Chuck's ear, I wondered if she was happy with all the changes I'd made on the farm. I knew she was glad I was here... and more importantly, I was glad I was here. I might make a lot less than I had in Houston, but I had made a good life for myself here, with good friends, work I loved (most of the time), and even a romantic relationship.

Although, if I was honest, the fact that Quinn and Peter were moving in together was a bit unsettling. Tobias and I had been together for quite some time, and we'd never talked about living together. As much as I loved him, I wasn't sure what I thought about sharing living quarters with my sweetie... and I wasn't sure what he thought about it, either. Would sharing a home damage what we had built together? Would he move to the farm? I knew I'd never leave the farm. Maybe I wasn't so different from Flora after all, I reflected with a bit of surprise. Giving up one's sovereignty wasn't something to be taken lightly. And could you have a long-term committed relationship without living together?

These were thoughts for another time, though. Tobias hadn't brought it up, and I wasn't about to, either. As I began drifting off, I heard the crunch of tires on the drive. I sat up, reached over, and flicked open the curtain over my bed. The headlights of a dark-colored dually truck coming down the driveway lit up the front of the Ulrich house as the vehicle pulled up beside the white Range Rover. The porch light came on and silhouetted a man in a baseball cap getting out of the truck and walking up the porch steps. He knocked, and a moment later the door opened and he disappeared inside.

I let the curtain drop, a little surprised that my tenant had a visitor—after all, she'd just arrived in Buttercup—and as Chuck nestled in behind my knees and Smoky curled up at my feet, I let sleep take me.

One of the things I'll never get used to with farm life is the morning milking.

It was barely light when I struggled out of bed, Chuck giving me a reproachful look. Lucky, one of my two kitty siblings, scooted up to the warm spot I'd just vacated, nestling up against the poodle. Chuck sniffed the air, yawned, and put his head back down.

"Must be nice," I said, reaching for a pair of shorts and tossing on an old Houston T-shirt before heading out to start the coffee.

By the time I had my boots on and coffee in hand, the sun was peeking over the horizon, gilding the world. The morning breeze rustled the leaves of the cottonwood and sycamore down by the creek, bringing a hint of coolness with it.

"Come on, girls!" I called; everyone was taking advantage of the cooler air to browse what was left in the pasture. Hot Lips, as usual, was testing the perimeter, with Blossom not far behind her; they hadn't escaped in months, but I knew better than to be complacent.

I stepped into the chicken coop to take care of lonely little Penny, feeling sad at the loss of my flock. I hadn't heard anything from the sheriff's office yet, but that was no surprise. I just hoped Niblet, Hester, and the rest of the girls, wherever they were, were okay.

By the time I got to the barn, Blossom, Hot Lips and the rest of the goats were all pushing to get in. The goats in particular had been a challenge to learn how to milk at first, and the cows were still easier, but we had settled into a routine with time, and although I wasn't going to be participating in any milking competitions in the near future (if such a thing existed), it no longer took hours every day. I got the sterilizing equipment, grabbed the food I used to keep everyone busy while I milked, and got to work, enjoying the breathing of the animals and the comforting rhythm of the milk hitting the pail. The smell of hay, the musky tang of the goats, and the breathing, living bodies felt primal; while milking had at first been my least favorite task, it was now one of my favorite parts of the day, except for the waking-up-early part. I finished with Hot Lips, who had been first in line, and moved on to Gidget, happy they were still producing despite the heat; there was definitely going to be lots of fresh chèvre for the market this weekend.

The heat had started by the time I let the last goat out into the pasture, grabbed the pails of milk, and headed toward the farmhouse.

I glanced down at the Ulrich house as I walked; the truck was gone, but the Range Rover was still there. And, unless I was mistaken, the front door was slightly ajar. Was Jo an early riser?

After stowing everything away in the fridge in the kitchen and putting down food for Chuck and the kitties, I decided to walk down to the little house and properly greet the new resident. I wasn't sure I was thrilled with the reason she'd come to Buttercup, but her rent payments were helping cover the farm's mortgage, and I couldn't afford to be churlish.

It was a short walk down to the Ulrich house, which was a ways toward the creek from the house. The house had had a reputation for being haunted, with loud noises coming from upstairs at night, but not long after moving it, we'd figured out the reason for the weird sounds, and it was harmless enough. I was glad I'd had a hand in rescuing the small wood-frame house, which was one of Buttercup's earliest homes and had a storied history, including a Comanche abduction of a former resident. Before settlement by Europeans, Buttercup had long been indigenous territory, most likely Tonkawa. I'd found what I suspected were a few stone tools along the creek bank, and there were several flint-knapping sites in the area. Although I'd grown up spending summers here, learning at my grandmother's knee, there was still so much about the land's history I was still uncovering. It was a mystery that kept unfolding, discovery by discovery.

But now there was another mystery to unravel. "Jo?" I called as I climbed the creaking steps to the front porch. The door flapped open, giving me a view of the small, blue-stenciled kitchen and the stairs, then swung shut with a bang that made me jump.

As I touched the door knob, a sudden whiff of lavender cascaded over me with the breeze, and goose bumps rose on my arms. There was no lavender blooming anywhere on the farm right now. Was my grandmother telling me something?

I paused for a moment, waiting for another breeze, but the air became suddenly still. I turned the door knob and pushed the door, taking a step into the little antique house.

"Jo?" I called again, scanning the small rooms. The kitchen was just as I'd left it after I'd cleaned, the countertops bare but for a coffeemaker and toaster, which looked like they hadn't been used yet, and to the right, beyond the stairs, the small living area was empty. The couch cushions had been squashed a bit, as if someone had sat there, and some file folders were scattered on the trunk I had turned into a coffee table. I checked the little bathroom tucked under the stairs, but the door was open and there was no sign of recent use.

Had Jo gone for a morning walk and not latched the door properly? I wondered. I didn't want to intrude, but something didn't feel right in the little house.

After one last scan of the living area, I moved back to the staircase and climbed it, calling Jo's name and hoping I wasn't disturbing her.

The two tiny bedrooms were on either side of the little house. The first hadn't been disturbed, but when I glanced into the other, I saw Jo sprawled on her stomach on the bed.

"I'm so sorry," I said, turning to backtrack down the stairs. She didn't move, though, and I noticed her arm dangling down off the side of the bed, completely motionless.

"Jo? Are you okay?" I asked.

Still no movement.

I approached the bedroom slowly, scanning the room. The suitcase was on the floor beside the dresser, and the closet door was closed.

She hadn't changed out of her work clothes; she was still in the gray suit I'd seen the day before. I sucked in my breath as I stood on the rag rug next to the bed. Jo lay on top of the quilt, her legs akimbo, her face buried in a pillow... and she was no longer breathing.

5

I hurried to her side, placing a finger against her neck. I nearly snatched it back—her skin was cold. But just to make sure, I searched for a pulse with one hand as I reached for my phone with the other.

Nothing.

I dialed 911, feeling heartsick. What had happened? Had she had a cardiac arrest, or a sudden stroke? Or had something else happened? I thought of the man in the truck as the phone rang.

I reeled off the situation to the dispatcher, who promised to send paramedics as soon as possible, then hung up.

The room was eerily silent. Jo looked like she was sleeping, but I knew better. I sat down on the rocking chair close to the door, keeping a kind of vigil as I waited.

Whatever had happened, Jo hadn't had a chance to unpack before she died. The only sign that she'd been here—other than her presence on the bed—was her unopened suitcase and a stack of papers on the antique dresser next to the door.

Out of curiosity, I got up and walked over to it. The top page said "Market Analysis": below was an address I recognized as belonging to Rosita's.

Using the hem of my T-shirt to avoid leaving fingerprints —just in case what had happened to Jo wasn't a result of natural causes—I flipped through the pages. Apparently the average rent in Buttercup had gone up rather precipitously the past few years, and Rosita's was paying below market value. And what Marcy had said about a Dallas organization being willing to move into the space hadn't been speculation; there was a line item for "proposed price per square foot" next to a chain restaurant's name, and the number was almost double what the Vargases appeared to be paying.

My stomach sank as I flipped through the rest of the analysis. Tucked in between the last two pages was a business card. Bitsy Hauser, a local real estate agent, was pictured, her blond hair sleek, her makeup impeccable.

As I studied it, wondering why Jo would have a card for a local real estate agent, I heard the sound of sirens. I took a quick picture with my phone — and then took a picture of the page with the chain restaurant's proposed numbers on it —and flipped it back closed, walking to the window.

~

UNFORTUNATELY FOR ME, Sheriff Rooster Kocurek was on duty today, and first on the scene, along with the paramedics.

I met him at the front door of the Ulrich House, finding myself unconsciously wrapping my arms around my body, as if that might somehow make me... I don't know. Invisible?

"What are you, some kind of Black Widow?" he asked, giving me a nasty look as the paramedics streamed past me.

"She's upstairs," I informed them as Rooster studied me. His belly seemed to protrude even more than usual over his brass belt buckle, and his polyester button-down shirt... well, let's just say the buttons were certainly being put through their paces. Rooster and his wife, Lacey, had been up and down the past few years, and Opal down at the station told me that during the down times, he had a penchant for Lone Stars, Dairy Queen Oreo Blizzards and triple Whataburgers. From the look of his buttons, I'd say things hadn't been great at home lately.

"Never been married, so I'm not exactly a widow." I'd had the unfortunate honor of finding more than one body in Buttercup. Rooster had fingered me as a murderer the first time we met, and I had the strong feeling he hadn't changed his opinion since then.

"Well, let's see if we're lookin' at a potential crime scene," he said, stepping up onto the porch and into the little house, with me following behind him. "How did you come to find this one?"

"I came down to check on her," I said. "She just moved in yesterday, and I didn't get a chance to say hello properly. The front door was open when I got here, and she didn't answer when I knocked..."

"So you just waltzed right in," he said.

"Her Range Rover's out front," I reminded him. "I was worried something might have happened to her."

"Hmmph," he replied, then, "wait here." I sat down on the love seat in the little living room as he lumbered up the narrow stairs to the second floor. I could already hear the creak in the floor from the paramedics.

As I studied the pretty blue stencil ringing the tops of

the walls (I had preserved it during renovation and it was one of my favorite things about the house), I heard Rooster's voice from somewhere above me. "How is she?"

"She's gone," a woman's voice responded.

"Heart attack or somethin'?" he asked.

"We'll have to wait for the coroner's report," the woman replied, "but see the burst blood vessels in her eyes? I'd put my money on asphyxiation."

"So not natural causes," Rooster said.

"Unless you consider being suffocated by a pillow natural, I'd say no. I texted the coroner; she should be out here soon."

Another murder, I thought, my heart sinking. And way too close to home.

"I guess we need to rope this off and consider it a crime scene," Rooster said, sounding deeply unhappy.

"That would be my recommendation," the paramedic said. "But like I said, I'm not the coroner." Her radio bleeped. "I think we're done here," she continued. "Can we leave the scene with you?"

"I'll wait for the coroner," he said. A few minutes later, the paramedics came down the stairs, nodded to me, and headed back out to the ambulance.

Rooster came down a minute later, his tread sounding even heavier than when he went up the stairs.

"Looks like we may have another murder on our hands," he said. "What time did you find her?"

"I don't know. Twenty, thirty minutes ago? Whenever I called."

"So you called right away?"

"Of course," I said.

"Touch anything?"

"Just her neck, looking for a pulse," I said. I didn't

mention the papers on the desk. My T-shirt had touched them, after all. Not me. "Any thoughts on who might have done it?"

"I don't know the first thing about that woman," he said.

"I don't know much either," I said. "Her name is Jo Nesbit. She's my short-term tenant, of course, but she's apparently representing Rosita's new landlord. She checked into the house yesterday, and was at Rosita's yesterday when I was having lunch." I decided not to tell Rooster about Rosita chasing Jo out of the restaurant with a cleaver; I figured he'd hear about that soon enough.

"So she's from out of town?"

"Dallas area," I said. "She booked the place for a month. She had a visitor last night."

"A visitor?" He narrowed his eyes at me. "But you said she just got into town yesterday."

"I thought the same thing."

"Did you see this visitor?"

"It looked like a man. He showed up at around ten or so, and was driving a truck."

"Late for a business meeting. What time did he leave?"

"The truck was there when I fell asleep, but he must have left sometime during the night, because it wasn't there this morning when I went out to do my chores. Speaking of chores," I said, "any word on the chicken-nappings?"

He blinked at me. "The what?"

"The missing poultry. My flock was stolen yesterday, and Opal told me I'm the third or fourth one this week."

"Oh, that." He waved my question away as if it were a pesky fly. "I've got one of the deputies lookin' into it."

"Well, I need my girls back," I said. "I'm worried what will happen to them if too much time goes by." I didn't like to think of Hester and Niblet turning up in somebody's stew pot.

"I've got other concerns, Miz Resnick," he said. "Like what happened to this lady in here. And how come you always seem to be at the scene of the crime. How did you know her, again?"

"I didn't," I said. "She booked the place online. I'd never laid eyes on her before yesterday"

"Right," he said, in a tone of voice that told me he wasn't convinced, and I felt my heart sink a little bit. "I'm going to head back upstairs," he continued. "Don't touch anything. In fact, you might want to go back to the main house."

"Sure," I said, watching as he lumbered back up the narrow staircase to the second floor. As I walked to the front door, I glanced into the small kitchen. The two wine glasses still stood on the dish-drying rack, both turned upside-down. Jo had shared wine with someone last night, and either washed the glasses before going up to bed... or whoever killed her washed the glasses before leaving, to eliminate any evidence.

Interesting.

TOBIAS ARRIVED right after the coroner left; when I called him, he'd cleared his schedule as quickly as he could and headed over to Dewberry Farm. He pulled in fast, causing little puffs of dry dust, and threw the truck door open, slamming it behind him. He glanced down at the Ulrich house as he trotted to the front porch, where I sat with a glass of iced tea, a concerned Chuck at my feet.

"Are you okay?" he asked as he hurried through the kissing gate and practically bounded over to me. I let him enfold me in a long, warm hug, my head against his chest, before answering.

"I am," I confirmed.

He hugged me tighter, then released me, looking into my eyes. "Tell me everything that happened."

I told him of the visitor I'd seen the night before, my discovery of Jo in her bed, what I'd overheard the paramedics say, Rooster's questions. "It doesn't make sense," I said.

"What?"

"Was this some kind of freak thing? Do I need to lock my doors and windows? Or did someone target her?"

"I think you absolutely should lock your doors and windows until we figure out what happened," Tobias said, "but you told me someone came to visit her and she let them in, so odds are good it wasn't a random thing."

"True," I conceded.

"Did anyone know she was here? Maybe it had something to do with what happened at Rosita's yesterday."

"I don't know if she told anyone local where she was staying. Anyway, it wasn't Rosita who came to visit her last night," I said. "And she definitely had at least a glass of wine with someone." I told him about the glasses I'd found in the dish drainer, and the empty bottle of wine.

"You think she had a glass with the man you saw in the truck?"

"It's my best guess," I said. "His truck was there when I went to sleep, and I didn't see or hear anyone else come down the drive."

"And you don't remember anything else about it?"

I tried to remember if anything had stood out to me. "It was a dark color. Not white or silver. And it was big. A dually."

"That doesn't exactly narrow it down, but it's a start," he said. "And the man himself?"

"I don't know," I answered. "It was too dark to make him out. I'm just curious who would be visiting her."

Tobias was about to say something when my phone rang. I looked down at it; it was Mandy Vargas. I turned the phone and showed it to Tobias.

"News travels fast," he said.

I picked up and greeted Mandy, but I had barely said "Hello" before she blurted, "I hear the representative of my parents' new landlord turned up dead at the Ulrich house."

"Hi, Mandy," I said. "And yes. I'm not sure what happened..."

"Asphyxiation, from what I'm told, but the coroner hasn't issued an official report."

"You are absolutely wasted on a small-town paper," I told her.

"One of the benefits of working in a small town is that nobody can keep anything secret," she said. "Makes my life easy. But I'm worried."

I could imagine why, but I let her keep going.

"My mom was... well, really upset with that Jo Nesbit woman when she came to the restaurant yesterday. The whole staff saw her threaten her. And now she turns up dead the next morning?"

"I get it," I said. "But did your mom even know where Jo Nesbit was staying?"

"Like I said, it's a small town."

"It is, but I'm the only one I know of who was aware she was staying at the farm, and I didn't know why she was here until I saw her drive up yesterday. And the only other person I told is Tobias. Except..."

"Except what?"

I told her about the man in the truck.

"A dark dually," she said. "That's not exactly a strong identifier in this part of the world."

"I know," I said. "If I'd known Jo was going to die, I might have paid more attention."

"You know Rooster's going to arrest my mom," Mandy said. "She's the obvious suspect."

"Not if she has an alibi," I reminded her.

"They go to bed at nine-thirty," Mandy said. "And she and dad don't sleep in the same room because he snores."

"Let's not jump to conclusions," I said. "It hasn't even been ruled a murder yet."

"Yet," she said, her voice laced with bitterness. "I need to get ahead of this. We need to find out everything we can about this woman. What was her last name?"

"She registered as Jo Nesbit," I told Mandy.

"I'm on it. Lucy... please, you've got to help me. With everything my mom's gone through this past year, I just can't let Rooster lock her up for something she didn't do."

"Mandy, we don't know what happened yet. And even if it was foul play, we know someone who wasn't your mother was at the Ulrich house last night. Surely Rooster's got to chase that down."

"I love your optimism," Mandy said gloomily. "But I'm going to go find out everything I can about that Jo Nesbit. Call me if you hear anything or think of anything, okay?"

"I will," I said.

"One last thing... what address did she give you when she registered?"

"She didn't," I said. "But I have a contact number." I looked it up on my phone and reeled it off to her.

"Thanks," she said. "Keep me posted."

She'd hung up before I could tell her I would.

6

Tobias had just left and I had just put a kettle on the stove to make a fresh batch of iced tea when I heard the crunch of tires coming up the driveway.

I glanced through the curtains. A black dually was rolling up to the farm, and adrenaline shot through me. Was the murderer coming back? Was I next?

I hurried to the front door to lock it as the truck pulled into one of the spaces in front of the farmhouse, and almost laughed in relief as my friend Molly Kramer hopped down from the driver's seat and shut the door behind her. She wore a flowered cotton dress I'd never seen before; she usually was a shorts and T-shirt kind of woman, particularly in such hot weather. Even though it was September, it still felt like summer.

"Molly!" I said, pushing through the door into the hot, dry air of the afternoon.

"I was hoping I'd find you here," Molly said, retrieving what looked like a pie from the front passenger side of the enormous truck and nudging the door closed with her shoulder. "I ran into Opal at the Red & White and heard what happened. Are you okay?"

"Better than my tenant, that's for sure," I said.

"Thank heavens," Molly said. "I brought peach pie. I figured you might need it."

"I love your peach pie," I said as she pulled me into a one-armed hug, then handed me the pie, which was brimming with juicy golden peaches and topped with a flaky lattice top that made my mouth water. Chuck, who had followed me out the door, also eyed the dish with interest.

"Not for you," I informed him. "Come on in," I told my friend. "I was just making a fresh batch of iced tea, but I still have some cold in the fridge. Can I get you a glass?"

"I'd love one," she said, following me into the kitchen and slumping into one of the kitchen chairs. "It feels good to sit down. Between the farm and the four kids, I feel like I could sleep for a month and still not be caught up."

Chuck, who had given up once I set the pie down, padded over and put his head on her leg, looking up at her with soulful brown eyes. "Awww," she said, giving his head a few strokes. "How did you know I needed some puppy love?"

He gave a contented sigh as I filled two glasses with ice, poured the tea, and garnished each with a mint sprig from the fridge. "How did your peaches come on this year?" she asked.

"I got a reasonable crop, actually," I said. "I just made jam from the last of them a few weeks ago. And now I'm ready for fall to start."

"Good luck with that. With the weather like this, it'll be a while before we get a proper fall." She glanced out the window at the sun-bleached pasture. The sun was high overhead in a cloudless sky and I could practically feel the heat radiating from the windowpanes.

"I know," I said as I set the glasses of tea on the table and then put a few oatmeal cookies from the cookie jar on a plate. "It's much too early for a blue norther. Still, a little tropical depression wouldn't hurt." I set the cookie plate on the table and sat down across from Molly. "Just some rain for relief. The creek's practically dry. There's still water in the well, and I'm trying not to use too much water to keep everything alive, but if it doesn't rain soon..."

"I hear you," she said, reaching for a cookie. "Alfie's out there checking the stock tanks every day, and worried about having enough hay."

"I haven't seen him in a while. How is he?"

Her mouth pulled to the side, and a small furrow appeared between her eyebrows. "Honestly? I'm a little worried about him."

"Why?"

"He just hasn't been himself lately."

"What do you mean?"

"He's been... quiet. And on his phone a lot. I've asked him what's going on, but he won't tell me."

"When did this start?"

She took a sip of tea and shrugged. "About a month ago. He says nothing's wrong, but I've been with him for twenty years, so I can tell he's not sharing everything with me."

"Everything okay at the ranch?"

"That I know of," she said. "He went out last night to check on a cow that's been having some trouble in the pasture we're leasing from the Froehlichs. He was gone for hours. I tried calling him when I got worried, but he didn't answer."

"What did he say when he got home?"

"He told me part of the fence was down, so he had to round up a few cows and fix the barbed wire. But he's usually so good about answering when he's out on the land. It just... I'm probably imagining things, but I'm nervous."

"What do you think it might be?" I asked, picking up a cookie and taking a bite of the chewy oatmeal.

She gave me a look that was filled with pain. "I... I hate to even suggest this," she said. "But I think he might be having an affair."

I practically choked on my cookie. After coughing a bit and washing down the crumbs with some tea, I put down my glass. "An affair? Oh, Molly... I just can't imagine."

"I know," she said, bursting into tears. "I never thought I'd be saying it. But he's just been so weird lately. I've tried to glance at his phone, but he always has it with him, and I don't know the passcode anyway." She swiped at her eyes. "I'm probably crazy."

"No," I said. "You've been married for twenty years. If your instinct is telling you there's something different, something wrong, I think you should trust it."

She let out a sad sigh. "That makes it worse, somehow."

"I get it," I said. "Have you talked to him?"

She gave a short, bitter laugh. "How? I've asked him if everything's okay a million times, and he always says yes. Am I supposed to just say, 'Are you seeing someone else?'"

"Would it be so much worse than sitting in misery wondering?" I asked.

"Honestly? I don't know," she said, taking a long sip of tea and reaching for another cookie. "I swear I've gained five pounds stress-eating. I can't even fit into my shorts anymore. That's why I'm wearing this," she said, pinching some of the flowered material of her dress between two fingers.

"I think it looks great, actually. Very boho, if that's the word I want."

"Thanks, I guess." She sighed. "I'll bet whoever she is is gorgeous and super-fit, just like Alfie. I probably should have made more time for the gym, but with the kids..."

"Hold it right there, missy," I said. "You are beautiful just as you are." And she was. The pink of the dress brought out the roses in her cheeks. Her silver-streaked brown hair was thick and slightly wavy, and her golden-brown eyes were fringed with dark lashes that accented their color.

"I'm in my forties," she said. "I'm nothing like I was when Alfie married me."

"You're better," I said. "Besides, you're jumping to conclusions."

"I guess I am," she said. She took another bite of cookie and chewed it slowly, staring out the window. Finally, she said, "Do I really have to ask him?"

"No, you don't," I said. "But you do have to tell him that his behavior is making you very worried and that you're starting to think he might be having an affair."

"Crap." She crammed the rest of the cookie into her mouth and followed it with the rest of the tea. "I guess you're right. But first I have to pick the kids up from school, start dinner, and get a mountain of soccer uniforms in the laundry so they're ready for the game."

"You're a great mom," I told her. "And a great wife. Just don't forget to take care of my friend, too."

"What do you mean?" she asked, grabbing another cookie and standing up. "Eating a half dozen cookies in ten minutes isn't self-care?"

I laughed. "You know what I mean. Just stop getting down on yourself. You are a total catch, and Alfie and the kids would be lost without you."

"The kids," she groaned. "What do I do about them if he is seeing someone else? I don't want them to grow up in a broken home..."

"Don't think about that. You have no idea what's going on until you talk with him."

She nodded. "You're right. Okay. I'll talk to him."

"Tonight?"

"I'll try," she said.

I stood up and pulled my friend into a big, long hug. "Call me anytime, okay? Whatever it is, I'm here for you."

"Thanks," she murmured into my hair, and I could feel her body relax a little bit in my arms." She pulled away then, ran her fingers under her eyes to clean up the little bit of smeared mascara, and took a deep breath. "Okay," she said, straightening her dress. "I'm off to be a mom again."

"And talk to Alfie as soon as you can," I said. "You don't want this hanging over you."

"I will," she said. "Thanks for the cookies and tea. And the pep talk."

"Anytime, Molly. And thanks for the pie," I told her. "Let me know how it goes, okay?"

"I will," she said, and together we walked out of my little farmhouse into the heat of the Texas afternoon. I watched as she climbed into the truck and headed down the driveway toward home.

As she turned onto the main road, I felt a little tug of apprehension in my stomach. Alfie's truck was a dark blue dually he'd bought a few years back... dark enough to look black after sunset. I walked over and looked at the tire prints in the dirt where Molly had parked and snapped a quick shot with my phone. Then I walked down to the Ulrich house, where yellow caution tape hung limp in the airless afternoon.

I looked down at the spot where I'd seen the dually park the night before, to the left of Jo's Range Rover. There were a lot of tracks now... after all, Rooster had pulled up next to the Range Rover when he arrived, and people had been in and out of the little house tens of times since last night.

But the dually had pulled up further than Rooster, and its tires were wide. There was only about a foot of clear tire track, but when I compared it to the picture on my phone, my stomach sank.

The tracks were a match.

"It could be a coincidence," Tobias said as he compared the photos on my phone that evening. We were sitting down at the table in my warm kitchen; my air conditioner was struggling to keep up with the unseasonable heat. "Lots of people get the same tires."

"I know," I said as I dished up some potato salad and then reached for the brisket; Tobias had picked up some Bubba's Barbecue on the way over, saving me from heating up the kitchen further. We were planning on Molly's peach pie with a scoop of ice cream for dessert. "But I know he wasn't home when whoever was driving that dually was here. And Molly says he's been off the past few weeks."

"Maybe he has been, but Jo only got here yesterday," Tobias pointed out, adding a pork rib to his plate. "I can feel my cholesterol going up already," he said. "But it'll be worth it."

I sighed and drizzled Bubba's homemade barbecue sauce over my brisket, then put on a few slices of sweet onion and dug in. The smoky, tender meat and the tangy sauce melded perfectly with the sweet-sharp bite of the onion, and I groaned aloud as I swallowed. "There really is nothing better than Texas barbecue, is there?" I asked, reaching for some iced tea to wash it down.

"Well, except maybe for Molly's peach pie," Tobias said. "We kind of hit the dinner jackpot tonight."

"We did," I agreed. "But I'm still worried about Alfie."

He took a sip of his own tea and set the glass down, looking at me. "You really think it was him here last night?"

"I don't know why, but I think we need to find out if he and Jo knew each other," I said.

"What do we know about her?"

"Nothing much yet. Only that she was working for a commercial real estate company out of Dallas."

Tobias wiped his hands with a napkin and reached for his phone. "Have you looked her up online?"

"I did a quick search this afternoon," I said. "All I could find was a LinkedIn profile that showed a bunch of Texas real estate jobs. She lives in Dallas."

"Right," he said. "Jo Nesbit?"

"That's it," I said.

He typed, and a moment later showed me a Facebook profile of a woman in dark sunglasses. "She lives in Dallas. No information other than a profile picture, and only seven friends."

"So not much there," I said. "I left a message for one of my old reporter colleagues. I'm going to ask her to see what she can find out."

"Maybe this Jo lady was having an affair with someone," Tobias suggested, jabbing a bit of mayonnaise-covered potato with a fork.

"Like Alfie?"

"No," he said. "Maybe a coworker from her firm. Or someone she knew in Dallas."

"It's an awfully long drive from Dallas," I said.

"Maybe she met someone online, and they're local?" Tobias suggested.

"I'm hoping so," I said. "Mandy Vargas is afraid her mother's going to be dragged down to the station. She asked me to help her make sure Rooster doesn't pin it on her."

"What if it was her?" Tobias asked.

"She doesn't drive a dually," I said. "And I doubt she'd stay for a glass of wine. Besides, I'm pretty sure it was a man I saw."

"Did anyone else come down the drive last night?"

"Not that I heard," I said. "And Chuck didn't bark, either."

"Hmm." He took another bite of brisket and chewed it slowly. "I saw Gus today," he said finally, when he had swallowed.

"Any news on the wedding?"

"We mainly talked about his cat, Buttons," Tobias said. "He's got a little tumor I have to take off and biopsy. But the topic of Flora did come up."

"Has she had a change of heart?"

Tobias shook his head. "Nope. Gus is heartbroken."

"Poor guy. It's a shame... they seemed so happy together. Did she really call it off because he wouldn't move into her house?"

"Apparently so," Tobias said. "And then Gus suggested they build a new house on her land, as a compromise, so their first house together would belong to both of them. Then she accused him of just marrying her for her money."

"Ouch. I guess she's still feeling wary after the last guy."

"Well, the last guy did try to kill her so he could inherit her fortune," Tobias pointed out.

"Gus isn't that way at all, though."

"I know," Tobias said. "I just wish she would talk with him. He says she's blocked his number and won't open the gate."

"Sounds like Quinn and I may have to try to do an intervention," I said. "I'll see her at the Blue Onion cafe tomorrow; maybe we can figure out a time to go visit Flora."

"Speaking of Quinn, how are the moving plans going?"

"She seems excited," I said. "And I think Pip is going to love having all that space to run."

"The goats aren't going to know what to do with him," Tobias said, grinning.

"I'm so glad Quinn found love again after everything she went through with Jed," I said, taking another bite of barbecue. My friend's abusive ex-spouse had inspired her to get a brown belt in martial arts to defend herself. Unfortunately, martial arts wouldn't do much to defend against a gun... and Jed liked his guns.

"I'm just glad Jed is locked up," Tobias said. "I know they've been apart for ages, but I would worry that finding out she'd moved on might stir him up again. How long is he still behind bars?"

"I don't know," I said. "I know he'll be up for parole at some point, but I'm not sure when." I shivered and I reached down to stroke Chuck's head, grateful that he—and Quinn and I—had survived our last encounter with Jed.

"At least she won't be living by herself," I said.

"I know," Tobias said. "I still worry."

"Let's just hope he'll have moved on by the time he gets out," I said. "In the meantime, I think I'm about ready for some pie. Can I get you a slice?"

"Is that even a question?" Tobias asked, biting the last bit of meat off a rib and getting up to clear the table.

7

The Blue Onion was bustling when I walked in at eleven the next morning. I waved to a few friends and pushed through the door to the kitchen, where Quinn had her arms elbow-deep in a tub of dough, the red bandanna around her head damp with sweat.

"It's almost as hot in the kitchen as it is outside," I said.

"The AC is on the fritz," Quinn said. "If you think this is bad, go upstairs; it's about 4000 degrees." She swiped at her forehead with the back of her arm. "I can hardly wait to move in with Peter full time."

"Are you still on schedule with that?"

"We're planning to move the last of the stuff on Monday," she said. "Pip's going to be so happy."

"And you?"

She smiled. "I am too," she said. "But enough about me. Tell me what's going on with the Ulrich house. I heard your tenant died."

"She did," I said. "What can I help you with while I talk?"

She gestured toward one of her young workers, who was busy making sandwiches at one of the counters. "If you could help Brittany get the orders out, that would be great."

"Brittany?" I smiled as she turned and gave me a little wave with a plastic-gloved hand. "When did you start working here?"

"Just last week," she said. "I'm saving up for a car."

"That's exciting!" I said.

"It goes so fast," Quinn sighed, looking at her daughter dreamily. "I remember when you got your first bike."

“I know, right? What can I do to help?" I asked Brittany.

"I'm on this ticket," Brittany said, pointing to the line of paper slips clipped to a line above the counter.

"As soon as I get this dough divvied up, I'll come help," Quinn said as she turned the bowl out onto a floured board and reached for a scale. "In the meantime," she said, "give us the skinny on what happened at your rental."

"Honestly," I said, looking sidelong at Brittany, "you know about as much as I do." I wasn't about to share my suspicions about Alfie Kramer with his daughter standing next to me.

"I hear she was some kind of real estate hotshot from Dallas," Quinn said. “Mary down at the Enchanted Florist told me she was working for a firm that was buying up cheap commercial properties and hiking up the rent."

"That sounds about right," I said, thinking of what happened at Rosita's. "There are at least a couple I know of myself. What have you heard about what properties they bought?"

"I think they got the old bank building across the way," she said.

"The one with Fannie's Antiques?" I asked.

She nodded. "Fannie told me the landlord just hiked the rent fifty percent when she went to renew. She's looking for another space now, but with all the folks moving away from the cities, you know how real estate prices have been." She plopped another chunk of dough into a bread pan and shaped it. "Even without a new landlord, the tax hikes are killing me. I'm kind of hoping I can talk the owner of this building into selling it to me so I can lock it in."

"Will she?" I asked.

"I don't know. I know the rent is funding her retirement, but I'm thinking if she'll finance it, I can take the whole thing over for her. These old buildings take work; between Peter and me, we can take care of most of it and save money."

"Is that part of the reason for the move?" I asked as I assembled a chicken salad sandwich and arranged it on a plate.

"It's part of it, but it's not the whole thing. We were spending so much time together it just seemed like the right next step. And it's hard when he stays over here, because he's got to get up before dawn to take care of things at Green Haven. Besides, he doesn't like to be away in case something comes up on the farm."

"I understand that," I said. "I was hit by the chicken-napper while I was at Tobias's; I wish I'd been home."

"Oh, no," Brittany said. "I heard that was going on. Dad put an extra lock on the chicken coop just in case. I'm raising a few hens for the county fair; they'd better not try to steal them." She scooped some potato chips onto a plate. "Maybe we should get a security camera."

"It's not a bad idea," I mused as I dished up some fruit salad. "Anyway," I said, returning to the topic of my late tenant, "have you heard anything else about this Jo Nesbit?"

"No," Quinn said. "But you might want to talk to Flora. You know Flora's mama bought all kinds of property around

Buttercup, and Flora mentioned somebody had recently reached out to her about selling some of it."

"I need to talk to her about the whole Gus fiasco anyway," I said. "I'll stop by when we're done here."

"No change regarding the wedding?" Quinn asked as she filled another bread pan and started sliding them into a covered rack to proof.

"Not that I know of," I said. "I'm wondering if there's more to the story than we know."

"Isn't there always?" Quinn asked as she put the last pan in and wiped her hands on a towel. "Now, then. Give me a ticket and I'll get started."

Brittany handed her the next one in line and we spent the next hour making sandwiches, slicing quiche, and dishing up salads.

IT WAS WELL over 100 degrees when I rolled up to Flora's front gate. I rolled down the window and hit the button on the intercom. Flora buzzed me in—I'd texted to let her know I was coming--and soon I was bumping down the long gravel driveway to the 1950s ranch house she'd shared with her mother for most of her life.

I surveyed the squat red-brick house, which was ringed with a tired-looking boxwood hedge that may have been as old as the house, and wondered why Flora had no interest in living somewhere a little more modern, or at least quaint.

I got out and walked up the concrete pathway to the front door, which was decorated with a faded wreath of what might once have been sunflowers, but now looked more like some sort of sea anemone. I had just reached for the doorbell when the door swung open.

"Thanks for coming to visit, Lucy," Flora said, ushering me into the tiled front entry. "I was just making a tuna casserole; you're welcome to stay for supper."

"Oh, thank you, but I've got to head back and take care of the farm," I told her. I loved Flora, but I hated tuna casserole.

“It’s good to see you,” my friend said. She’d reverted to her pre-Gus wardrobe, I noticed; today she wore a drab olive-colored T-shirt that hung on her bony frame, along with a pair of loose jeans that looked like they might have been bought thirty years ago.

“I’m really sorry about you and Gus,” I said. “It’s too bad you two aren’t together; you seemed so happy!”

“I thought we were happy,” she said as she led me to the linoleum-floored kitchen. “Tea?” she offered as she gestured me to the kitchen table.

“Yes, please,” I said. “So what happened?” I asked as I slid into a chair at the table.

“He wanted to build some kind of huge mansion,” she said, retrieving a pitcher of tea from the refrigerator. “So we could live in it together.”

“And?” I asked.

“That’s it.” She grabbed two glasses from the cabinet and put them down on the counter, hard. “I’ve spent my whole life in this house. I don’t need a fancy kitchen, or a swimming pool, or any of that.” She sloshed tea into the glasses. “I thought he loved me for me. Now I’m realizing it was just a ploy.”

I was quiet as she shoved the tea back in the fridge and plunked two glasses on the table.

“I can see you’re hurting,” I said.

“I’m not,” she said flatly. “I’m over him.”

I took a sip of tea and let silence sit in the air for a moment. “Was there anything else?” I asked.

She looked at me. “Isn’t that enough? He was marrying me for my money,” she said. “I just didn’t know it. I was such a fool. Again.” Her voice broke. “Mother was right. Nobody is going to love me. They’ll just want to use me.” As she spoke, her face crumpled, and although she was in her fifties, I could see the hurt little girl from all those years ago.

“Oh, Flora,” I said, pulling my chair over to her and putting an arm around her as her body heaved with sobs. “Your mother was wrong. You can’t let her keep running your life this way.”

“Really?” she asked, bitterness in her voice. “She was right about Roger. I told her she was wrong, but she wasn’t. And this time, I finally let my guard down, and what happens? The same thing.”

“The same thing?” I asked gently. “I don’t understand how it’s the same thing. Can you explain?”

“I told you,” she spat. “This house...” she gestured around at the dated kitchen, with its peeling floral wall-paper above the kitchen window and the harvest-gold refrigerator humming loudly in the corner. “He refuses to live here. It’s been good enough for me for more than fifty years, and for my mother before me. If he can’t live in this house with me, then he must not love me.” The argument was childishly simple, but to her I could tell it had the ring of finality.

“So he said he won’t move into this house after the wedding?”

She shook her head. “Nope. He had an architect draw up plans for some kind of big modern place out back some-where.” She gestured somewhere behind the house. “Built with a lot of my money, of course. And he didn't even consult me before he did it."

"That really upset you."

"Of course it did!" she said. "I finally saw his true colors. Now he's saying he'll move in here, but I can't trust him anymore. And how can I marry someone I don't trust?"

"He hurt you."

"He did," she said. "He went behind my back. He didn't even talk to me about it."

"Did he apologize?"

"I guess," she said with a dismissive shrug. "But like I said. It's too late."

I sighed and took another sip of tea. "Are you sure? I know there's no way to understand what's going on in a relationship from the outside, but from what I saw, Gus really seems to love you."

Her eyes narrowed. "I appreciate your concern, but my mind is made up," she said, and I could almost feel her tucking away her feelings and zipping herself back up. Living with an overbearing mother like Nettie Kocurek for most of her life had taught her to hide her emotions. Nettie might be gone, but she was still firmly in control of her daughter's life.

"All right," I said. "I can tell the subject is closed for now."

"Forever," she amended.

"I get it," I replied, and decided to change the subject. "I wanted to find out how you were doing, of course, but I also have a question for you... you heard about the woman who... uh, passed away in my rental house?"

"I did," she said, and her face relaxed a little. "What about her?"

"I heard she came and asked about buying some of your

property," I said. "I was wondering if you could tell me what you thought of her."

"Are you investigating her death?" Flora asked. "Did someone murder her?"

"I don't know if the coroner's made that determination yet," I replied, "but it did look kind of suspicious, and I'm trying to understand a little more about who she was and what might have happened."

"Well," Flora said, leaning back in her chair and crossing her thin arms over her chest, "she struck me as an opportunist. And a bargain-hunter."

"Did she give you a low-ball offer?"

Flora nodded. "And a list of all the problems with the property. Roof needed to be replaced, she said. Cracks in the masonry. Would cost half a million dollars just to restore it, but she'd be happy to take it off my hands for half that and put in the work herself."

"How kind of her," I said dryly.

"Exactly," Flora said. "And here's the thing. She even dredged up some old stories about the building. Told me there were rumors of bad luck, and a ghost."

"I've never heard that before," I said.

"Fortunately, I have no interest in selling," Flora said. "But this Jo woman told me she dug up information on Mary McIntosh; she owns her own building, the one that The Enchanted Florist is in. You know Mary has had some medical issues the last year... breast cancer, I think, and insurance didn't cover all of it. She missed a few payments during chemo and got in trouble with the mortgage company. So you know what Jo's outfit did?"

"What?"

"They bought the mortgage and then sent her a foreclosure notice for late payments."

"So they foreclosed on her?"

"It's set to happen in three weeks," Flora said, "unless Mary can pay the note off. She's livid."

"I'll bet she is. That's terrible!" I said.

"It is. She's put so much time and resources into that business over the years, and it gives her the income she's needed to supplement her social security."

"What happens now that Jo is dead, do you think? Will the foreclosure go through?" If not, I thought, that would certainly give Mary a good reason to want Jo out of the way. Who knew I had been hosting such a cruel opportunist?

"I don't know," Flora said with a shrug. "I guess it depends on who's running the company."

"What's the name of it?"

"New Horizons, New Day, something like that." She pursed her lips. "You know, she looked familiar to me somehow."

"Who? Jo?"

Flora nodded. "I feel like I've seen her before, but I can't think where. I mean, I've hardly been out of Buttercup my whole life. But there's something about her... that's why I looked into her operation and discovered what she was about."

"I'm impressed you found all that out. Mandy asked if maybe I might want to write for the Zephyr, but your research skills are terrific, Flora."

She looked up, her cheeks pinking slightly. "Really? Mama always told me I wasn't much good at anything."

"Mama didn't know what she was talking about," I said. "She was blind when it came to how amazing you are." I took another sip of tea. "I hate to beat a dead horse, but I really think you should give Gus a second chance."

Her face began to harden, and I held my hand up.

"Wait," I said. "Let me finish. I've never seen you happier than when you were with Gus. My instincts with people are good, and if I thought he was after you for your money, I'd be the first person to tell you."

Her lips formed a thin line.

"I'm not saying go back to him right now," I said. "I'm saying maybe think about it. And talk to him. You're both gutted over this, and I think it may just be something you need to talk about."

"Is that all?" Flora said shortly. "Because I'm just not up for this conversation right now."

"I understand," I said, finishing my tea and standing up. "I just felt like I needed to tell you what I see. Will you at least think about it?"

"My mother was in charge of my life for 52 years," Flora said, venom in her voice. "I'm done being told what to do."

I took an involuntary step back; I'd never seen this kind of anger from my friend before. "I get it," I said. "It's just... I want what's best for you."

"Thank you for your input," Flora said. "Now, if you'll excuse me, I have work to do."

I was dismissed.

8

Twenty minutes later, I was knocking on the door of the *Buttercup Zephyr* and admiring the coral geraniums Mandy had planted in pots by the door. A hummingbird darted to and from a glass feeder hanging from the end of the porch, zooming away when the young woman opened the door.

"Whatcha got for me?" she asked without preamble.

"Some less-than-savory business practices, for starters," I said.

"Come on in," she said, and I was grateful for the cool rush of air conditioning after the heat of the summer afternoon. "Tea?"

"I'd love some," I told her, following her to the little kitchen in the back of the old house that was the home of the local paper. The grass in the small back yard was brown and dry, but a lone Esperanza bush by the back porch was alight with yellow bells, one of the few things blooming after the long, hot August. Bees moved industriously from one yellow bell-shaped flower to another as I sat down at the little kitchen table.

"Rooster questioned my mom this morning," Mandy said, a furrow between her brows. Dark circles ringed her eyes. "Suspicious death, he's calling it. I called the coroner's office; the woman I talked to told me off the record that it looks like the victim was suffocated."

I sighed.

Mandy poured two glasses of tea and sat down across from me at the table, pushing one in my direction. "Usually, I'd argue my mother was too weak to do something like that, but she lugs fifty-pound bags of masa harina around all the time, so she's a bit of an exception."

I turned my glass around on the table. "He's really serious about charging her?"

"I don't know," Mandy said with a tired shrug, "but I know she threatened the victim in public that day, and everyone else in Buttercup has heard about it by now, I'm sure. The woman wasn't a local, so there's not a very long list of suspects." She took a long swig of tea. "Anyway, tell me what you found out."

"Well," I said, "you know how commercial mortgages work, right?"

"They're adjustable-rate, right? Not like residential mortgages."

"Right," I said. "And since interest rates went through the roof, a lot of folks are getting hit with a lot bigger bills for their mortgages."

"I know. It's no wonder everything's getting more expensive."

"That's part of it. But what's also happening is that people like Jo are going after small property owners who are behind because they can't keep up with the new, bigger bills."

"How are they going after them?" Mandy asked.

"Well, they find distressed mortgages—those that have a few missed or late payments—buy the loans from the original lender, and then move to foreclose on the owner."

"Actually, I think that's what happened to the owner of the Rosita's building," Mandy said. "I know she couldn't keep up with the bills after the taxes and the mortgage went up. She talked to my mom about raising the rent, but she couldn't, because there was another year left on the contract."

"When does your mom's lease expire?"

"In about three months," Mandy said. "Which is when the rent pretty much doubles." She took another sip of tea. "My parents have owned that restaurant my whole life. I don't know what they're going to do if they have to close." She gave a bitter laugh. "Of course, if my mom's in jail—or worse—for a murder she didn't commit, we've got bigger problems than my parents' retirement to worry about."

"Let's hope it doesn't end up there," I said. "Anyway, Flora told me that Jo has been poking around Buttercup looking to make more deals. Rosita's isn't the only business that's under the gun."

"If they were, then someone else in Buttercup would have a motive," Mandy said.

"Exactly," I said.

She sat up a little straighter. "You said someone was there that night."

"Yes, but it was dark," I said. "I couldn't recognize them."

"A dark dually, I thought you said."

"Yes," I replied. "But I wasn't really paying that much attention, to be honest. I wish I had, I didn't realize it would be important."

"Right. Do we know anything else about Jo Nesbit?"

"Flora said she looked a little familiar to her," I said.

"She tried to buy some of Flora's land for cheap. Flora shut her down, of course."

"Shame about Flora and Gus, by the way," Mandy said.

"I know. I'm working on it."

"Good luck," Mandy said. "She sounded pretty done last time I saw her. Anyway, back to Jo. I searched the records for her name, but I didn't turn anything up in the area."

"Maybe Nesbit is her married name," I suggested.

"That's a possibility. Have you checked out her social media?" Without waiting for an answer, she pulled out her phone. After a moment, she grimaced. "Nothing much, is there?"

"Nope," I said.

Mandy sighed. "Why Buttercup, I wonder?"

"Property values have gone way up here recently," I said. "Why not? Maybe her company's hitting lots of small towns."

"Maybe," Mandy said, but she didn't look convinced. "Flora said she looked familiar?"

"She did," I said.

"How old was Jo?"

"I'd put her in her mid- to late-forties," I said. "Why?"

"I'm wondering if maybe she was in Buttercup when she was younger. Feel like looking through some yearbooks with me?"

"You think maybe she went to high school here?"

"It's just a hunch," Mandy said, "but we might as well look." She pushed her chair back. "I've got copies of them in the back room. If she's mid-to-late forties, that would put us back what... thirty years, right?"

"That makes sense to me."

"I'll be right back," she said, and scurried off.

I watched the bees in the Esperanza as I waited; they

moved from blossom to blossom methodically, collecting nectar and honey. The heat didn't seem to bother them one bit. The hummingbird had just come back for another shot at the feeder when Mandy returned to the kitchen with a banker's box.

"I brought about ten years worth," she said. "It'll go fast if we're both looking. All right, let's start with her name."

It didn't take us long to figure out that there had been no Jo Nesbit in Buttercup in the years we were looking at; indeed no one at all with the last name of Nesbit.

"That was a washout," Mandy said. "But like you said, maybe she had a different last name as a kid. We'll have to look at the pictures and see if we can find someone who looks like her. Let me bring up a photo of her again, just so we remember what she looks like."

She picked up her phone and quickly found the LinkedIn photo, which showed Jo tastefully made up, her dark hair coiffed and her lips dark glossy red. "I'm sure she's changed, but it's something to go on. She's got dark hair and... brown eyes," she said, zooming in on the photo.

She took one slim, hardbound yearbook labeled Buttercup Broncos from the top of the stack we'd finished with, and then took another one herself.

"Anything starting with a J, right? Josephine, Joanne, Jordan..."

"That's what I'm thinking," Mandy said. "You never know."

I leafed through the first yearbook. The only Jo was a Jo Beth Ulrich, who was blonde with pale blue eyes.

"Definitely not," Mandy said. We went through four more, coming up with no vaguely possible options, and I was about to say we should hang it up when Mandy said, "I think I've got something."

I looked up from the FFA section of the yearbook I was perusing. "Show me."

"It's hard to tell, but here's a Jody Karbach that could be our Jo." She turned the yearbook around and pointed to a picture of a large-toothed girl with severe bangs and very thick glasses. She was ducking her chin slightly, as if she were embarrassed to have her photo taken.

"It's kind of hard to tell," I said.

"I know, but look at the chin. And then there's this mole here next to her mouth..."

She turned her phone toward me so I could compare the two faces side by side. The picture of Jo had a mole in what looked like the same place, just above her upper lip.

"I think you may be right," I said. I looked at the yearbook page again. "Is that Alfie?" I asked, pointing to a picture of a fresh-faced, square-chinned young man with a shock of dark hair. A fresh wave of misgiving washed over me.

"It sure is," Mandy said. "He was a looker in high school, wasn't he?"

"He's still a handsome man," I said. "Is Molly in here, too, then?"

"What's her maiden name?"

"Galuska, I think." I flipped through the pages until I found my friend's familiar face. Even though decades had passed, I recognized her infectious smile and laughing eyes.

Mandy pulled out her laptop as I looked at my friend's old photo, wondering what the connection was between Alfie Kramer and Jody Karbach... and if it had anything to do with what had happened to Jo Nesbit in the Ulrich house.

"Okay," Mandy said, pulling me from my less-than-pleasant reverie. "Let's see if we get any hits on Jody

Karbach." Her fingers flew over the keyboard, and a moment later, she looked up at me and grimaced. "Nothing other than a lot of ads for search services."

"No social media?"

She shook her head and hit another return key. "Nope. Wait... there's one thing. An obituary."

"For whom?"

"A Jimmy Karbach. Jody's listed as a survivor." Mandy cocked her head. "I heard about that; I was a little young, but I remember folks talking about it."

"What happened?"

"Somebody shot him with a hunting rifle in his deer blind. His daughter is the one who found him, if I remember right."

"Oof. Did they find out who did it?"

"They never did," Mandy said. "He wasn't very popular around here—apparently he wasn't very nice to his wife and liked to woo some of the married ladies—so the general consensus was that his wife or an angry husband had enough and did him in. There weren't any real clues—or at least none that anyone identified—and eventually the sheriff ruled it an accidental death, some kind of stray bullet from another hunter. But everybody in town figured someone had it in for him."

"When did this happen?"

She looked at the date of the obituary. "The same year as this yearbook," she said. "The funeral was March 13."

"I thought hunting season was over by March."

"I think it usually ends in February, which makes the hunting story not very believable," Mandy said, and sighed. "The Kocureks may have been sheriffs here for generations, but they've never been the sharpest blades in the drawers."

Something about the story piqued my curiosity. "Can

you find copies of any articles in the *Zephyr* about his death?" I asked.

"Why? You think it might be related to what happened at your place?"

I shrugged. "I don't know, but since I don't have anything else to go on, it's worth considering."

"Good idea," she said. "I'll see what I can find in the archives this afternoon. I'll scan copies and send you what I find." She sighed. "Not that we'll find much. I'm guessing law enforcement wasn't much different then than it is now." She gave me a grim look. "Which is why we need to find out who really killed Jo Nesbit—or Jody Karbach."

"If Opal was around, maybe she could fill us in on anything that isn't in the papers, too." Opal, who pretty much ran the sheriff's office, was often a goldmine of information. I didn't know how long she'd been in that job, but I'd gotten the impression she'd started young and never left. "I'll call some of my old friends at the *Chronicle* on the way home and see if they can dig anything up. Marriage records, employment..."

"I'll look on my end, too," Mandy said. "And you might want to talk to the Kramers when you get a chance," she suggested. "See if they remember anything about Jody."

I was uncomfortable at the thought of it, but I knew I needed to do exactly that—and ask Alfie if he had been the one at the Ulrich house the night Jo died, and what he was doing there.

"I will," I promised. "Can I borrow this yearbook?" I asked.

"Of course," she told me. "And keep me posted!"

9

I pulled up the road to Dewberry Farm about half an hour later; chores awaited me, not least making sure all of my vegetables weren't all shriveling to death in the heat.

They were, of course, and I spent an hour moving and running irrigation hoses, picking cherry tomatoes and eggplant, and harvesting some basil. Then I checked on Blossom and the goats; they were all huddling in the shade of the barn, looking morose. "I know," I told them. "I'm hot, too."

Hot Lips gave me a long-suffering look, as if to remind me that at least I had access to air conditioning, and I refilled their water tank, giving everyone a spritz from the hose to cool them off, before heading inside.

As Chuck did his business near my grandmother's rose-bushes in the front yard, I set the tomatoes and eggplant on the counter and did a mental inventory of my dinner options. I had fresh mozzarella in the fridge and garlic in the garlic keeper on the counter; if I made a batch of pasta, it would be delicious with chopped cherry tomatoes, basil and olive oil, mixed with some garlic and diced mozzarella. Quick, easy, and delicious. I'd roast an eggplant once the sun went down and it wasn't too hot to turn the oven on, so I'd have that for lunch tomorrow with the leftovers.

Once I had sorted dinner in my head and let Chuck back inside, I poured myself a glass of tea and sat down at my grandmother's kitchen table with the yearbook. Chuck flopped at my feet, panting as if he'd run a marathon, and Lucky and Smoky batted at his wagging tail as I reached down to scratch behind his ears.

I flipped through the pages, scanning for familiar names and faces. I knew I needed to talk to Alfie about Jo—or Jody, as it were—but I didn't want to do it until I was sure they were the same person... and if there was someone else who might remember her, I wanted to touch base with them first.

I went through several pages before finding a few familiar names. Frank Poehler, down at the Hitching Post, was there, along with Mary McIntosh of the Enchanted Florist. That was interesting, I thought, in light of the fact that the Enchanted Florist building was one of the targets of the late Jo Nesbit.

IT WAS a little late in the day for a trip to The Enchanted Florist—and late in the growing season, to boot—but I was always game for a visit to anything having to do with plants. Besides, plants weren't what I was in the market for, anyway. I needed to know if Jody Karbach and Jo Nesbit were in fact the same person.

I pulled up in one of the diagonal parking places on the

square right outside the little building Mary had turned into a botanical wonderland. The old brick building, which was over a hundred years old, bordered an empty lot, so in addition to the cut flowers she kept inside, an array of native plants and gorgeous garden flowers created the appearance of a lush English garden, even with the punishing heat.

After tucking the yearbook into a canvas bag and slinging it over my shoulder, I let myself in through the small gate, disturbing a bumblebee who was collecting nectar and pollen from a trumpet vine blossom. The dusty sweet scent of crape myrtles perfumed the air, and even in the heat, bursts of lantana exploded in swathes of gold, crimson, and lavender, alongside deep purple verbena and the tall, pink-flowered spires of obedient plant, a Texas native.

As a light breeze stirred, tinkling the wind chimes hanging from the side of the building, I walked past a line of rosemary starts, brushing my fingers along them and inhaling the woodsy, herbal scent. A few flats of zinnias in a rainbow of pinks, reds, and oranges blossomed by the door to the shop, alongside an array of pink and magenta gomphrena... always a hot weather bloomer.

Exercising an impressive amount of restraint, I pushed through the door to the cool florist shop without picking up a single plant, much less a flat of the zinnias I'd been coveting. It was too late in the season to plant them without watering multiple times a day—and besides, my budget didn't extend to ornamental garden plants at the moment.

The bells on the door jingled as I closed the glass-paned shop door behind me. The inside of the Enchanted Florist was every bit as beguiling as the exterior, with creative arrangements of lilies, delphiniums, roses, and even peonies (which didn't grow in Texas, alas) scenting the cool air.

I was bending down to sniff a creamy white lily when Mary emerged from the chilled room behind the counter, wearing a green smock over linen shorts and a faded T-shirt. A cut rose was in one work-roughened hand, a pair of clippers in the other, and a green bandana covered her head.

"Long time no see, Lucy," she said. Her face, lined from years out working in the garden, looked thinner than usual, the lines in her forehead and around her mouth deeper than I remembered.

"I've been busy and short of cash, and you know your store is like a candy shop for me. I can never resist."

She grinned. "I totally understand. I'm just the same way."

"Everything here looks amazing as always," I told her.

"Thanks," she said. "It's been hard lately, as I'm sure you know."

"I heard you've been having some health issues, yes," I said.

"And landlord issues, too." She grimaced. "In fact, I'm not sure how much longer I can keep the doors open."

"I heard that, too," I said.

"Although considering the recent events out at your place," she said, "maybe the process will be a bit delayed and I can figure out some other plan."

"You mean the death of Jo Nesbit?"

She nodded. "She's ruthless, that one. Not a compassionate bone in her body." She rubbed her fingers together. "It's all about the money."

"I wanted to ask you something about her, actually." I pulled the yearbook from the canvas bag on my shoulder.

"What's that?"

"Your yearbook from Buttercup High," I told her, flipping through to the picture of Jody Karbach.

"What does this have to do with the building?"

I set the yearbook down on the front counter and pointed to the picture of Jody. "Do you remember her?"

"Who, Jody?" She blinked. "I knew her, of course—we knew everyone—but we weren't exactly friends."

"Who was she friends with?"

"She was only here for a few years," Mary said. "She came for high school; her dad got a job on one of the ranches here, so her family came and stayed. They rented a mobile home somewhere toward LaGrange, I think. Why?"

"Did she stay after high school?"

She shook her head. "I don't know where she went. I'm afraid we weren't very welcoming to her, now that I think of it."

"No?"

"She was always a little... different. Kind of kept to herself, socially awkward. Good grades, though. She was smart, and a hard worker, but not someone we really invited to parties or anything." She looked at the picture again, and then at me. "Why are you asking me about Jody Karbach?"

I pulled my phone out of my pocket, pulled up the picture of Jo Nesbit, and set it next to the yearbook photo. Mary looked confused for a moment, and then her eyebrows shot up. "Jo... Jody! No wonder she looked a little familiar!"

"You think it's the same person?"

"It is, I'm almost sure of it," she said. "Jody had this habit of twisting a lock of hair around her index finger," she said. "Jo did the same thing. And her voice... the way she spoke, kind of flat-like. She looked so different, so much prettier with her hair done up the way it is now, and so much more confident... I never would have made the connection, but I think you're right."

"She didn't mention knowing you?"

"No, not at all," Mary said. "Which is kind of weird. Why wouldn't she say something?"

"Maybe she didn't think you'd like her very much?" I suggested.

"Well, I absolutely don't like her very much. She's trying to steal my building." She crossed her arms over her chest and grimaced. "Or she was, anyway. I guess I just spoke ill of the dead. I'm not supposed to do that, am I?"

"I think you'll be forgiven in this case," I said. "At any rate, I've been wondering if Jo—or Jody—might still have some connections in Buttercup. Do you remember who she hung out with in high school?"

"Not really," Mary said. "We ran in different circles. I think I remember everyone teasing her because she had a crush on Alfie Kramer ever since ninth grade."

"Oh?" I said, heart sinking. The last thing I needed to hear was that Alfie and Jo had a history. Although it sounded awfully one-sided.

"She used to follow him everywhere; once she even went to his house at night, peeking through his bedroom window. Alfie's father threatened to shoot her if she came by again."

"She was a stalker, then."

Mary nodded. "And she did NOT like Molly once she came on the scene, I'll tell you that."

I was sure she didn't. But if her attraction to Alfie wasn't requited, what was he doing at the Ulrich house the night she died—if it had been him? Had there been something after all... and had it been rekindled?

Was Alfie the reason Jo came back to Buttercup? "Were Alfie and Molly dating even back then?" I asked.

"It was pretty much love at first sight with those two,"

Mary said. "They started dating in tenth grade and have been together ever since."

"Did Alfie ever talk to Jody when they were at school? I mean, Jo? Were they friends?"

Mary shook her head. "No. And it got worse after Jody's father died in that hunting accident."

"I heard about that."

"It was pretty ugly after that. People started to say that she was the one to do it... but Alfie stepped up and defended her. I always wondered about that."

From what I knew of Alfie, that sounded like something he would do; Molly told me he had never taken kindly to bullies, and I believed her. "What did he say?"

"He said that people were jumping to conclusions, and that Jody was innocent."

"She never was arrested?"

Mary shook her head. "No. But everyone in town thought she was involved. He wasn't a nice person; he drank too much, spent as much as he earned, and was a womanizer. Rumor was he got a little rough sometimes, too." She frowned. "It must have been a hard home to grow up in. Anyway, Jody got a job after school at the Red & White to help pay the rent, even before he died."

"Where was her mother?"

Mary shrugged. "I don't know. As far as I know, it was just the two of them, Jody and her sleazy father. And then it was just her." She grimaced. "I feel bad about it now. I should have been more supportive. We all should have. But you know how kids are..." She let out a bitter laugh. "And she managed to get her revenge anyway, didn't she? She put me into foreclosure."

"So you're thinking her return to Buttercup wasn't just business?"

"No, ma'am," Mary said, shaking her head. "Now that I know who she was, and I can put two and two together? I think Jody Karbach came back to Buttercup to settle some scores."

"Wow," I said, looking down at the yearbook pictures. All those fresh, bright faces. Yet even then, there was darkness.

"What's going to happen now that she's gone?" I asked. "I mean, with the building?"

Mary shrugged. "I don't know. But it should slow things down at least, maybe give me a chance to figure something out." She looked around at the flower arrangements, the light pouring through the front window and gleaming on the hardwood floors. "I've put my whole life into this place. I'd do anything to keep from losing everything I've built."

Anything? I wondered.

Including murder?

MY NEXT STOP was the Red & White grocery. I needed to pick up a bit of flour and baking powder for the kitchen, but I also wanted to see if Edna Orsak remembered Jody Karbach.

I was in luck; parked behind the register near the front was Edna, who had been running the store with her husband since (as Quinn once put it) dinosaurs roamed the earth. Business was slow today, so she was staring hard at her phone, jabbing at it with a finger.

"Hi, Edna!" I said.

"Hold on a moment... let me finish this level of Candy Crush... okay," she said, looking up from her phone. "What can I help you with, Lucy?"

"I need to pick up some baking supplies," I told her, "but I also had a question."

"Does this have something to do with that lady you found dead in your rent house?" she asked with a knowing look in her eye. "She was in here yesterday, actually. I wasn't, but one of my new hires checked her out, and he told me he saw her just hours before she... well, before she checked out, so to speak."

"When was that?"

"Mid-afternoon," she said. "Grayson said she bought two bottles of wine, a wedge of brie and some crackers..." She glanced over her shoulder, then whispered in a theatrical voice, "and a box of... prophylactics."

"Oh my," I said.

"Oh my, indeed. Sounds like she was expecting company if you ask me," she said. "Although I'm guessing things didn't turn out the way she expected."

"Unfortunately, I'm guessing you're right."

Edna adjusted her necklace, a gold chain with a turquoise cross that nestled above her ample cleavage. Edna's employees wore red T-shirts with the Red & White logo, but Edna preferred deep V-necks; today's was a bright teal that was just a few shades deeper than the turquoise on the cross. "That's got to give you the heebie-jeebies," she said. "It happened just fifty feet from where you were sleeping! The Ulrich house already has a reputation... I know y'all decided that the racket there wasn't anything to worry about, but maybe there's more to it after all." She was referring to our discovery that the noise made by the "ghost" in the Ulrich house was actually the result of the metal roof contracting as the temperature dropped.

"I hope not," I said. "I've got enough troubles as it is. Actually, though, that's not what I came in to ask you about."

"Huh," Edna said. "Well, then, what can I do you for?"

I pulled the yearbook out of the bag again and opened it to the page with Jody Karbach's picture. "Do you remember her?"

Edna searched next to the register for her readers, then put them on and leaned in. "Jody Karbach. Of course I do. She worked here for a couple years, when she was in high school."

"What do you remember about her?"

"Well, she had a huge crush on Alfie Kramer, that's for sure," she said. Apparently everybody in Buttercup knew about that, I thought. Small towns can be tough.

"How did you know?"

"Turned beet red every time he came in and forgot how to use the register. Plus, Alfie's dad caught her peeping through the windows." She shook her head. "Shame about her father, though. After he passed, she took as many hours as I could give her. I gave her a little extra, too, just to help her get by."

"That was kind of you," I said.

"I had to make it on my own for a few years when I was a girl," she said. "Kind folks helped me from time to time, when they were able; I like to pay that forward when I can."

"I love that," I said. I had no idea Edna had been on her own when she was young... or that she had such a kind streak. "It sounds like you liked Jody."

She nodded. "She was awkward, and I know those kids at the high school were none too kind—she and her dad were poor as churchmice—but I tried to make her feel at home here. After all, her mama was gone, and she had no kin."

"What happened to her mother, anyway?"

"She never said," Edna told me. "I gathered she took off

when Jody was just a little thing." She peered at the photo again. "Poor thing. I wonder what happened to her, anyway?" She looked up at me. "And what does she have to do with anything? Is she moving back to Buttercup?"

"I think she was already here," I said. "I think Jo Nesbit is Jody Karbach."

10

"Shut the front door," Edna said, eyes wide. "So this Jo woman who wound up dead is the same person as little Jody Karbach?"

"Seems so," I said.

"I heard the sheriff thinks Rosita Vargas did her in. Something about Jo wanting to close her down."

"Where did you hear that?"

"Oh, people talk all the time when they're shopping," Edna said with a shrug. She looked down at the yearbook photo again. "Poor little Jody. I can't believe she came back after all these years. Only to have this happen... it's so sad!"

"I know," I said. "I was wondering if you have any idea why she *did* come back. It doesn't sound like her time here was very good."

"No," Edna said, "I don't think it was. The only thing I can think of is maybe she was carrying a torch for Alfie Kramer?"

"Then why come back and start buying up distressed properties?" I asked. "Why not just send him an e-mail and invite him out for coffee?"

"Maybe she was worried Molly wouldn't like it."

"I'm sure she wouldn't," I said, "but do you think maybe Jody came back to exact some kind of revenge on people who weren't very nice to her in high school or something?"

"Rosita's older than Jo," Edna said. "They weren't in high school together."

"No, but Mary McIntosh down at the Enchanted Florist went to school with her. And Jo's trying to foreclose on the building."

"She and Mary never did get along," Edna said, pursing her lips.

"Who else do you remember Jo—Jody—not getting along with?" I asked.

"Hmm," Edna said. "I remember her getting into it with one of the popular girls, but I can't think who it was."

"What happened?"

"The girl—she was a cheerleader, but I can't remember which one right now—came in after having a few drinks one night. Jody was on the register. Anyway, she came right up to Jody and told her she knew she'd shot her no-good dad herself and gotten away with murder."

"What did Jody do?"

"Well, she was in the process of ringing up a bunch of yogurts. But instead of putting them in the bag, she just started throwing them at the girl. I remember them bursting open, she threw them so hard. The girl ran out of the store with strawberry goo in her hair, crying. But if you ask me, she deserved it."

"Do you think Jody had anything to do with what happened to her dad?"

"Her dad was a bad egg, but he was all Jody had. She loved him. She didn't talk for a month after he passed."

"Did she ever say what she thought might have happened?"

Edna shook her head. "She shut down anytime we brought it up, so we just acted like everything was normal and nothing had happened." She sighed. "I probably should have been better about that."

"It sounds to me like you helped her in the most important way."

"What, with the extra hours?"

"And the extra money."

"I guess. I still can't help feeling I shoulda done more. Anyway," she said, fingering the cross on her chest, "that was a long time ago. I can't imagine anyone would want to do that poor girl harm all these years later."

"Unless maybe she knew something about someone?" I suggested.

"Like, she was goin' to blackmail someone?" Edna asked, giving me a speculative look from over her readers. "She had money, or at least she must have had access to it, if she was comin' into town buying everybody out. Why would she need blackmail?"

I shrugged. "Maybe she was looking for payback," I suggested. "Maybe she stirred something up."

"Like what?" Edna asked.

"I don't know," I said. "But I'm guessing maybe she had some unfinished business from back then."

"Poor girl." Edna shook her head. "I'm so sorry she came to such a bad end, just like her father did."

"You mentioned he was a 'bad egg.' What did you mean by that?"

"He... well, he was a good-looking man. And he liked the ladies. Didn't matter to him if they were married or not."

"Ah," I said.

"He wasn't a good father, either," she added. "I know for a fact that poor girl spent a lot of nights at home on her own. Couldn't afford a car, so she rode her bike home at night. And her work here paid most of the rent; he was a drinker. Always down at the Hitchin' Post, drinkin' whiskey."

"Did any of the husbands find out their wives had been... well, had been unfaithful to them."

"Some of them did," she said. "Which made it even harder for the poor girl at school. Especially when..."

I waited as her eyes darted around, as if looking to make sure we couldn't be overheard.

"Fred Green caught his wife Alice in bed with Jimmy Karbach the week after Thanksgiving one year. Told him he'd kill him if he ever saw him within a hundred feet of his wife again. He was furious." She lowered her voice further. "Only reason they didn't divorce is that he was raised Catholic, but the marriage was never the same after that."

"I can imagine," I said, processing this new information about Alice Green. She was a prominent member of the local Catholic Church, and she had raised a lot of money for the needy—including Bessie Mae, a local woman whose family had been in Buttercup for years and who lived in the old train station—but the few times I'd met Alice, I'd gotten the feeling she was one of those women who thought there were two ways to do things: her way, and the wrong way.

"Well, her daughter Bitsy came down on Jody like a ton of bricks. She's got a twin—was Alfie's best friend at the time, actually—but Bobby is the quiet one of the two, never said much about what had happened. Bitsy, though? She wanted Jody gone from Buttercup permanently; I think all the talk of what happened with her mom embarrassed her."

"Are Bobby and Alfie still friends?" I'd never heard Molly or Alfie talk about anyone named Bobby.

"I don't know," she said. "They were thick as thieves at the time, but after high school, he and Bobby kind of drifted away from each other. He still lives in town, does accounting work, I think, but kind of keeps to himself." Edna sighed. "It was a real mess. Bitsy was never quite the same after what happened with her parents."

"How long before the hunting incident was the affair discovered?"

"I think it was just a couple months before Jimmy checked out for good, if you know what I mean. It's a sad story. Do you really think the killer's someone here in Buttercup?" Edna asked. "And who do you think she was buying those... well, you know, for?"

"I was wondering the same thing," I said. "Did she date anyone when she was in high school?"

Edna shook her head. "Not that I can remember. And she should know this town is small enough that everyone and their dog would know she bought what she bought. Most folks go into LaGrange to buy things they don't want people talkin' about."

"Maybe she figured no one here in Buttercup knew who she was, so it didn't matter," I said. Or else, I added mentally, she didn't mind someone finding out.

Had she been planning a rendezvous with Alfie? And if so, had she wanted word of it to get back to Molly?

As I wondered again why Jody had come back to Buttercup incognito, the door opened and Alfie Kramer walked in. He looked, as usual, like Buttercup's answer to the Marlboro Man; he was tall, rangy, and the kind of handsome that spoke of a lot of time outside doing physical labor. It wasn't hard to understand why Jody had had a terrible crush on him... and why Molly married him.

"There he is!" Edna said before I could stop her. "Lucy

and I were just talking about that woman who wound up meetin' her maker down in the Ulrich House. Turns out she was Jody Karbach. Isn't that somethin'?"

Alfie came to a complete stop, and his easy smile evaporated. There was an awkward silence as he regained his composure, but the smile didn't return, and his eyes darted to me before settling back on Edna. "Well, I'll be," he said. "What brought her back to Buttercup after all this time?"

"That's what Lucy and I were just speculatin' on. I was tellin' her about that crush she had on you. Boy, she had it bad, didn't she?"

"That was a long time ago," Alfie said quietly.

"It was, wasn't it? She thought you hung the moon, and would have given her eye teeth to be your girlfriend, but Molly had you all wrapped up from the start."

"I had no idea she was back," he said. "Shame she passed." His eyes flitted to me again. "Any word from the sheriff on what happened?"

"Not yet," I said. I knew I needed to ask if he'd been by the farm to visit her the night she died, but with Edna standing three feet away and hanging on every word, now was definitely not the time. I also had no idea how to broach it. "Did you run into her at all while she was here?"

"Nope," he said. "Anyway," he continued, "Molly sent me out to pick up some milk for dinner, so I'd better get on. Good to see both of you; hope you can come to dinner again soon, Lucy."

"I'd love that," I said, more cheerily than I felt. "Say hi to Molly for me when you get home."

As he nodded to both of us and strode past us toward the dairy case in the back, Edna's eyes followed him. "I certainly can understand what she saw in him. I've always said he was a tall drink of water. Heck, if I was a couple decades younger, I might have gone after him myself." She gave me a conspiratorial grin. "Don't mention that to my husband, though, will you?"

I laughed. "Of course not."

"You didn't do too badly yourself, now that I think of it. Dr. Brandt is a catch for any woman." She smiled at me and said, in a conspiratorial tone, "Any weddin' bells on the horizon for you two lovebirds?"

"We haven't really talked about it," I said, feeling uncomfortable with the topic. We hadn't discussed formalizing our relationship... and I wasn't yet sure where either of us came down on it.

"Well, you know my vote. We could use a good wedding in town. Sad about Gus and Flora. I keep hopin' they'll patch it up."

"Me too," I said. "I tried talking to her, but she seems kind of dug in."

"Once burned, twice shy, I guess."

"But Gus is nothing like Roger."

"I know, I know. Maybe she'll come to her senses."

"Maybe," I said, gloomily.

As I spoke, Alfie came up behind me. His normally easy smile was nowhere to be found.

"Isn't that something, about Jody Karbach?" Edna said to him. "Sad story, isn't it?"

"It is," he said, putting the milk down by the register. "Anyhow, I'd love to stop and chat, but I've got my marching orders from Molly."

"Got it," Edna said, ringing him up. He handed her a ten dollar bill, and she darted him a flirtatious smile as she counted his change. "Say hi to that pretty wife of yours for me."

"Will do," he said, nodding to both of us before heading

for the door, looking anxious to put distance between him and us.

"Wonder what's eatin' him?" Edna said, watching him as the glass door closed behind him.

I shrugged. "I don't know, but I should probably do my own shopping before it's time to take care of the next round of chores. Thanks for filling me in on Jody."

"Sad business," she said, shaking her head. "I hope they find out who did it."

"Me too," I told her.

I just hoped it wasn't anyone I knew and cared for.

11

I had just gotten home and put my groceries up when the phone rang. I picked it up; it was Quinn.

"I'm in!" she said.

"You moved out? I was going to help you!"

"Oh, we decided to go ahead and do it early, what with the A/C problems over at the apartment. Anyway, I was calling to see if you and Tobias could come for dinner soon."

"I'd love to," I said, "but let me check with him."

"Got it. Any news on what happened to your tenant? Or your chickens?"

"Nothing on the chickens," I said, thinking of poor lonely Penny and making a mental note to go check on her as soon as I got off the phone. I wondered what had happened to the rest of my flock; I missed their antics, and made a note to call Opal as soon as I got off the phone. Jo (or Jody's) death had dominated my attention, but I did love my girls, and I wanted them back. "But I did find out a lot about Jo."

"So did I," she said. "Which is part of the reason I called."

"Oh? What do you know?"

"About a week ago, she was down at the Hitchin' Post."

"That doesn't surprise me," I said. After all, she'd apparently been busy in Buttercup for a while. "Was she with anyone?"

"She was," Quinn said. "And I don't know what to make of it."

"Who was it?"

"Well, again, I'm just hearing this from my friend, so I wasn't there, but she says she saw her talkin' with Alfie Kramer."

My heart sank. "Did she hear anything?"

"No," she said. "But Alfie seemed upset, from what she told me. He walked out of the place in a hurry."

"Hmm," I said. "Anything else?"

"Just that," she said. "What did you find out?"

"Apparently she went to high school here in Buttercup," I said. I told her what I'd learned about Jody's infatuation with Alfie, and the difficult events she'd endured as a teenager in Buttercup.

"That sounds really rough," Quinn said. "Small towns can be great, but when everyone knows your business, it can be tough, too. Especially when you're a teen."

"I'll bet."

"If she had a massive crush on him in high school," Quinn said, "maybe she was still carrying a torch and hoped he'd reconsider."

"She did upgrade her look," I said. "At least based on the high school yearbook photo I saw."

"That would explain why she was talking to him."

"But he was married. And if her crush really was unrequited, why was he in touch with her at all?" I asked.

"Maybe he didn't know who she was. Maybe she lured him to the bar under the guise of wanting to make a business offer or something?"

"That would explain why he left in a huff, I guess." But it didn't explain why he'd come to the Ulrich house the night Jody died—if it was him.

"Does Molly know who she was yet?" Quinn asked.

"I don't think so," I said. "And I don't want to be the one to tell her."

"Have you talked with Alfie about it?"

"No," I said. "I ran into him at the Red & White today—apparently Jody used to work at the store back in high school, and Edna was telling me about her. Alfie came in, and she told him we'd figured out Jo was Jody."

"Oof. How did he react?"

"He got out of there in a hurry," I said. "I got the impression he didn't want to discuss the topic."

"That doesn't sound suspicious at all," she said with a sigh. "Gus and Flora, and now Molly and Alfie... It's almost like something's in the water."

"You and Peter seem to be doing okay," I pointed out.

"True," she said. "How about you and Tobias?"

"We're fine as far as I know," I said.

"Good," she told me. "Oops... I've got to run... let me know about dinner when you talk to Tobias!"

"I will," I said. As soon as we hung up, I dialed Opal down at the sheriff's office.

"Lucy!" she said. "How's everything at Dewberry Farm?"

"Well, my chickens are gone, I'm short a tenant, it's a million degrees and we haven't had rain in weeks, but other than that, it's business as usual."

"Ouch," she said. "Are you calling about Jo? Or the chickens?"

"Either. Both. Any news?"

"Well, you know I'm not allowed to talk about police business with civilians," she said, then lowered her voice. "But it definitely wasn't accidental," she said. "And Rooster is on his way to the Vargases later on tonight."

"Oh, no," I groaned. Poor Rosita. "Doesn't she have an alibi?"

"I sure hope so," she said. "I guess we'll know more by tomorrow."

"Any word on Jo's background yet?" I asked.

"Nothing. No next of kin we can find. We're waiting to tell the news outlets until we can find out who her family is."

"I can tell you that right now," I said. "Her original name was Jody Karbach. I don't know what happened to her mother, but her father is no longer with us."

"Jody Karbach?" she breathed. "I remember that name. Her daddy died in that huntin' accident couple of decades past. Sad story. They never did find out who pulled the trigger."

"Two murders in one family," I said. "Think they could be connected?"

"Well, Lucy, I don't know how they could be. She was just a slip of a girl when she lost her daddy, and all those years have gone by..."

"It's worth considering, I think."

"Rooster won't like it," she said. "You know how he likes an open-and-shut case. But I'll tell 'im."

"Do you still have the case files on her father's death?"

"I'm sure they're here somewhere," she said. "It wouldn't

hurt to take a look at them, see if anyone missed something, I suppose."

"I'd appreciate it if you did," I told her. "Anything more on the chickens, by the way?"

"Not a peep," she said. "Sorry for the bad pun. This whole thing with Jo Nesbit has kinda taken over the office, but I'll make sure Rooster remembers it."

"Thanks, Opal. Let me know if you find out anything."

"Of course, Lucy," she said. "By the way, if you've got any more of that dewberry jam you brought me a few months back..."

I laughed. "I'll drop a jar by tomorrow."

"Thank heavens. I'm almost out!"

12

Dinner at Green Haven was always a treat. Tobias was planning to come over to Dewberry Farm late that afternoon after he finished up at the vet clinic, and we would head over together. In the meantime, I was finishing up chores and making ice cream to take with us to dinner; I'd thawed some of the dewberries I'd picked and frozen earlier that summer, and decided that a no-cook dewberry ice cream would be just the thing for a hot summer day.

I'd picked the last of the straggling zinnias and put them in a vase on the table, moved irrigation hoses for the zillionth time that summer, and just pulsed the thawed berries in a food processor with sugar and some lemon zest. As I waited for the berries to marinate a bit, I poured myself a glass of iced tea, grabbed a hat from a peg by the door, and headed out toward the Ulrich house.

A hot breeze greeted me as I shut the door to the farmhouse; it was like being hit by a giant blow dryer. By the time I crossed the crispy grass and stepped onto the front porch of the little house by the creek, the skin on my face felt tight from the heat and I was covered in a sheen of sweat.

The police tape was gone; someone had retrieved it while I was out that day. I wondered if that meant I'd get a call from Mandy soon, telling me her mother had been arrested.

The front door creaked as I opened it, and I stepped into the cool interior with relief, making a mental note to turn the temperature up now that the little house was uninhabited.

The interior was much as it had been when I found Jo. The wine glasses were gone from the kitchen, though, along with the empty bottle; I imagined they were now in an evidence locker somewhere. Would they find Alfie's DNA on one of them? Not on the glasses, they'd been washed, but the wine bottle perhaps? Would they be able to trace it back to him if they did?

My heart was heavy as I walked around the little living room, thinking about what had happened here while I was a short distance away in my little yellow farmhouse. I really needed to talk with Alfie soon; I knew in my heart he had been here that night. He was married to one of my closest friends, and I needed to know what had happened between him and Jo.

I walked up the narrow staircase toward the bedroom. Why would someone want to kill Jo now? From what I'd heard, she had had a crush on Alfie, not the other way around. But if that was the case, what was Alfie doing here drinking wine while his wife thought he was somewhere else? And would the threat of Jo saying something to Molly be enough motive to silence her permanently?

It wasn't adding up.

I looked again at the bed where I'd found Jo, still

wearing her business clothes, and reviewed everything I'd learned in the short time since Jo's death.

She'd definitely had a history here in Buttercup, and not a good one. Was it bad enough that she'd come back to exact revenge on some of her high school classmates? Had her threat of foreclosure on the Enchanted Florist been enough to cause Mary to snuff her out? Was there someone else in town who was facing dire consequences because of her... someone who wasn't yet on my radar?

I walked over to the bed and sat down on it, looking out the wavy glass window at the rolling Texas countryside. A hot breeze swept the dry meadow outside, and the little house creaked as the air swirled around the clapboard walls. I felt like I was missing something important here... but I wasn't sure what.

A cool breeze unrelated to the scirocco sweeping the pasture outside stirred my hair, and I caught the scent of lavender. The door of the wardrobe on the far wall swung open a few inches, and I shivered.

I eased myself up off the bed and crossed the room to the wardrobe. Inside, a short row of tailored jackets and skirts in sober blue and gray hung on a rod, along with a few silk blouses. Not exactly the ideal wardrobe for a Texas summer, in my opinion, but based on her personal history and her current real estate mission in Buttercup, I could understand why Jo would tend toward power attire. I looked at the base of the wardrobe to see if there was anything there, but other than a few pairs of heels, it was devoid of anything interesting.

I was about to close the doors again when the scent of lavender intensified. What should I be looking for?

One by one, I examined the jackets. The pockets were sewed shut, as was normal for women's clothes, and the skirts, likewise, were devoid of any practical storage. I was looking at the last jacket when I noticed a leather purse slung over the neck of the hanger.

Glancing over my shoulder as if someone might be watching me (which was a little ridiculous, really), I opened the clasp of the small leather handbag.

Inside was a tube of lipstick, a compact with the Chanel logo emblazoned on it, and a folded up piece of newspaper that looked like an article someone had snipped.

I tucked the makeup back into the purse and opened up the news article, which was yellowed and had evidently been folded and unfolded so many times that the paper was soft and had worn thin in the creases.

I wasn't surprised to read the headline: "Local Man Killed in Hunting Accident."

It was an article from the *Buttercup Zephyr*, of course, and the "local man" was Jo's father, Jimmy Karbach.

I read through it, although I was already familiar with the details—a hunter's stray bullet had hit Jimmy in the deer blind at the back of the property he was renting, and the sheriff's office was treating it as an accident.

I tucked the article into the back pocket of my shorts and continued to poke around the wardrobe, but there was nothing else.

A few minutes later, I retraced my steps downstairs, more convinced than ever that Jody Karbach hadn't just come back to Buttercup to make a quick buck.

She'd had unfinished business, too.

~

BACK IN THE FARMHOUSE, I strained the berries to remove the seeds, then returned the dark, juicy pulp to the food processor and added heavy whipping cream. When the cream had turned a rich berry hue, I paused the processor, plugged in the ice cream maker I'd found at a thrift shop last spring, and removed the canister insert from the freezer, filling it with the creamy mixture and positioning it before hitting the start button. As the machine whirred, turning the berry mixture into ice cream, I sat down at the table and looked at my phone. I really couldn't put it off any longer.

I scrolled through my contacts list, then hit "dial." The phone rang four times, then went to voicemail.

"You've reached Alfie Kramer," came the familiar drawl from the earpiece, and my stomach twisted yet again. "Please leave a message, and I'll get back to you as soon as I can."

I took a deep breath, and after the beep, I said, "Hi, Alfie, it's Lucy. I need to talk to you about something. Please call when you can." I paused for a moment, then added, "It's about Jody Karbach," and hung up.

My heart was racing as I sat at the kitchen table. Would he call me back? What would I do if he didn't?

13

Despite the crushing heat, Green Haven was just like it sounded; a green and cool haven. Peter's home, a gorgeous, rammed-earth structure that reminded me of Bag End in *The Hobbit*, was cloaked in Virginia creeper and passionflower that, despite the heat, were still vibrant. A swath of zinnias and sage flanked the hand-tooled wood front door.

Pip bounded over to greet us as Tobias and I pulled up in one of the parking places next to the fence; a moment later, the front door opened, and Quinn emerged, grinning.

I grabbed the cooler that housed the dewberry ice cream and a bottle of Texas white wine Tobias and I had brought back from a winery near Fredericksburg and greeted my friend, my heart a little bit lighter to see her so happy.

"Did you bring Chuck?" she asked as she opened the gate and hugged me.

"He stuck his nose out the door, decided it was too hot, and plopped back down in front of the fridge, I'm afraid," I said as Pip galloped circles around us, then sat at Tobias's feet.

"Good boy!' Tobias said, bending down to rub behind the wagging black lab mix's ears.

"We brought a bottle of wine and dessert," I said, offering Quinn the cooler.

"Perfect! Peter is just finishing dressing the salad. Come on in!"

Tobias and I followed her into the little house, which smelled deliciously of cooking garlic.

Peter stood at the butcher block counter, tossing a salad in a wooden bowl. "Thanks so much for coming over and helping us celebrate!" he said, pausing in his preparations to give each of us a hug.

"We wouldn't miss it," Tobias said.

"Can I get you a glass of wine?" Quinn asked, retrieving the bottle from the cooler.

"That would be great," I said. "We should probably put the ice cream in the freezer, too."

"Ice cream? Is that what I think it is?" Quinn asked, peering into the cooler.

"I used the second to last bag of dewberries just for you," I said, grinning.

"Oooh, I can't wait," she said, as she put the bowl into the freezer.

"I can't wait to eat whatever it is *you're* making," Tobias said to Peter.

"Ratatouille," he said. "With goat cheese, of course, pasta... and Quinn's homemade bread."

"It smells wonderful," I told him, and looked around the homey kitchen as Quinn opened the wine and poured us glasses.

We sat down at the table, and Peter joined us a moment later, setting down a pan of cooked vegetables smattered with creamy goat cheese, a hand-thrown bowl of fresh farfalle, and the salad he'd just dressed. Quinn brought the basket of her fresh, crusty bread and a pot of butter, and we dug in with relish.

"What's in this, anyway?" Tobias asked as he forked up some pasta and ratatouille. "And how do you make it?"

"It's just lots of summer vegetables. Zucchini, eggplant, of course... peppers and onion and plenty of garlic, all chopped up and sautéed in some of the olive oil I got from one of my farmer friends near Dripping Springs."

"What about the tomatoes?" I asked. "They taste so fresh."

"I cut them up and douse them in balsamic vinegar, then add them at the end, along with some butter, then toss in goat cheese and basil at the very end."

"I could eat this every day," I said. "Can you give me the recipe?"

He laughed. "I just did. It's not hard, I promise."

I looked over at Quinn, who was buttering a piece of bread. "I can see why you decided to make the move, my friend."

"It's just one of many perks," she said, giving Peter an affectionate smile. He reached over and touched her shoulder. "We finished cleaning out the apartment today," she said.

"What's the landlord going to do with it?" I asked.

"I don't know yet," Quinn said, smile fading. "Like I told you, I'm still hoping that maybe I can buy out the building. If she were to sell it to someone else, I'd be in trouble. I'm a little bit worried."

"Lots of that going on lately, it seems," Tobias said.

"Yeah. Apparently that Jo Nesbit lady was part of it... I heard she was trying to buy up half of Buttercup."

"Or foreclose on it, anyway," I said, and told her about Mary down at the Enchanted Florist.

"That's horrible," Quinn said. "Why would someone do that?"

I took a sip of my wine, which was delightfully dry and fragrant. "I think Jo had a bit of an ax to grind in Buttercup."

"Why? I thought she was from Dallas," Peter said.

"That's where she ended up," I said, "but she went to high school in Buttercup, at least for a couple of years, and from what I've heard, it wasn't a fabulous experience."

"How come everyone I talked to thought she was an outsider, then?" Quinn asked.

"Her name was different," I told her, then recounted everything we'd discovered about Jo Nesbit, nee Jody Karbach, since I'd found her in the Ulrich House.

"I've heard revenge is a dish best served cold, but twenty years is a long time," Peter said.

"And she didn't get to eat it anyway," I said.

"I wonder what she stirred up?" Quinn asked.

"A hornet's nest, it sounds like to me," Tobias said. "I wonder if she was planning on foreclosing on anyone other than Mary's Enchanted Florist?"

"We need to find out who else's mortgage got bought by Jo's company," I suggested. "I'll ask Mandy to look into it."

"How are Rosita and her family holding up, anyway?" Peter asked.

"Well, Rooster's been asking her questions, so I think odds are good he's looking at her as the prime suspect."

"Do you think it's possible she did it?" Peter asked.

"I don't think so," I said. "I have a feeling there are a lot more people in town who had it out for Jo." I speared a piece of eggplant and a farfalle and escorted the duo to my mouth, wishing I had some answer to the question of what had happened to Jo. Preferably an answer that didn't involve Alfie Kramer.

"Enough about that," Quinn said after a long silence. "Any news on Flora and Gus?"

"No change, I'm afraid," I told her. "I tried to talk to her the other day, and she pretty much booted me out the door. Thank goodness you two are happy, at least!"

"We are," Peter said, giving Quinn an adoring look that made her positively glow.

I finished the last of my ratatouille and my wine, topping it off with a piece of Quinn's warm bread, then leaned back in my chair. "That was delicious."

"I hope you saved room for ice cream," Peter said as he stood up to clear the table.

"Let me do that," Tobias said. "You two cooked."

"Tobias is right. I'll help," I offered.

"All right," he said. "I'll let you clear," he told Tobias, "and maybe Lucy can dish up the ice cream?"

"Happy to!" I said, and a few minutes later we were all seated again, with bowls of creamy, velvety dewberry ice cream in front of us.

"This is heaven," Quinn said as she spooned a biteful into her mouth. "I need this recipe for sure. Is there lemon in it?"

"A touch of lemon zest," I said.

"It's just right," she told me. "I could eat this three meals a day and still not get tired of it."

"I completely agree," Peter said. "We need to plant more dewberry vines this fall, I think."

"If fall ever comes," Quinn said. We all glanced out the window at the sunbleached world outside. Although the leaves of the pecans by the little house were still green and the branches heavy with soon-to-be-picked nuts, the grass was the color of straw, even in the glow of the fading sunset.

"It may come a little later than it used to, but it will," Tobias said. "Before you know it, Peter and Lucy will be out at ten o'clock at night covering everything up so it doesn't freeze."

"Or spraying everything with baking soda like we did earlier this year, after we got powdery mildew from too much rain," Peter said.

"Farming is always an adventure, isn't it?" I laughed.

We spent the next hour lingering at the table. Night had fallen, and Peter and Tobias had just poured themselves small glasses of Texas-made bourbon when Pip, who had been lounging under the table hoping for scraps, sat up and began to growl.

"What is it?" Quinn asked sharply, suddenly alert. Although her ex, Jed, was behind bars and couldn't hurt her, her time with him had left its mark on her... she was always alert for danger.

Peter stood up. "I don't know, but we're going to find out."

"I'll go with you," Tobias said. As he spoke, there was a squawking sound from outside. Peter grabbed a flashlight and baseball bat from the closet by the front door, choked up on the bat, and hurried out the door with Tobias and me in his wake.

14

Tobias wielded the flashlight, and the beam bounced as we ran toward the squawking noise, which came from the tree-covered corner of the farm where Peter kept his chickens.

The light illuminated a dark figure carrying what looked like a bundle of feathers. I saw the paler oval of a face turn toward us, then whoever it was sprang into a run.

"Stop!" Peter called, but the intruder didn't break stride. We were still twenty yards away when the beam of the flashlight caught the flash of a door closing. A moment later, red taillights flared, an engine roared to life, and the flashlight caught the back of a pick-up truck with the Ford logo emblazoned on the tailgate and what looked like a large cage in the truck bed bouncing away across the pasture toward the gate.

Peter swore as the truck receded into the darkness, passed through the open gate and turned onto the road.

"I got the first three digits of the license plate," Tobias said. "XQC."

"I'll write that down," I said, pulling up my phone. "Ford pick-up. Any idea what model?"

"I'd say about ten or fifteen years old," Peter said. "I just hope they didn't get all of my girls."

"I'll go close the gate while you two check on the chickens," Tobias offered. "Take the flashlight; I'll use the light on my phone," he said, handing me the flashlight.

"Thanks," Peter said. "I can't believe this is happening. Who the heck would steal chickens?"

"All but one of mine were stolen a few nights ago," I said.

"Quinn told me about that," Peter said as we got to the open coop. He flashed his light inside. Where normally the roost was lined with feathery bodies, now it was empty, and only about a half dozen ruffled chickens paced the dirt floor, looking agitated. "Oh, no," he said. "They got Girly Girl, and Love Chick, too."

I grimaced. "I'm so sorry, Peter."

He did a quick headcount. "They took fifteen of them. Damn."

"Maybe now that we have a partial license plate, we have a chance at tracking them down," I said. "At least we have a lead."

"I guess," he said, and cooed at the remaining chickens in a soothing voice. "It's all right, girls. I'll get a padlock on your coop; I probably should have put one on a few days ago."

"Do you have one?" I asked.

"I do," he said with a sigh. "I just can't believe I have to lock my chickens up in Buttercup."

"I know," I said, feeling a pang as I wondered where my own chickens had disappeared to... and if I would be able to find them in time.

Quinn was anxiously waiting for news when we got back to the house.

"Everything okay?" she asked. She was standing in the front hall, hands up in front of her as if she were about to start a karate sparring match. Pip sat next to her, ears alert, still on guard.

"It was the chickennapper," I said.

She winced. "Oh, no! Did you catch them in time?"

"Not before they got Girly Girl and Love Chick," Peter said. "They managed to steal fifteen of the girls before we surprised them."

"We did get a partial license plate, though," Tobias said. "And we know it's a Ford truck."

"Maybe now the police will do something about it," I said.

"I hope they get on it fast," Quinn said, shivering. "I just wonder sometimes if I'll ever feel safe," she added, her face pale.

"Oh, sweetheart," Peter said, coming up behind her as she dropped her hands. "I've got you. That's why you're here... you can relax. I won't let anything happen to you."

"I... thank you," she said, turning to bury her face in his chest as he put his arms around her and stroked her curly hair. "I'm so sorry," she said. "It's just... sometimes I think I'll never be able to put what Jed did behind me."

"It's okay, love," Peter murmured into her hair. Tobias and I exchanged looks. We were both worried about Quinn.

"I called the station, and they said they'll send someone out to investigate," Tobias said. "It won't be till morning, though, most likely. Why don't I go with you and get the padlock on the coop?"

"That would be good," Peter said, looking at me. "Will you stay with Quinn?"

"Of course," I said. "Come on," I said to Quinn as Peter released her from his arms and she swiped at her eyes, looking embarrassed by the tears that streaked her face. "I'm going to get a start on the dishes; you can keep me company."

"No," Quinn said, taking a deep, shaky breath. "You can keep *me* company; you're our guest, after all."

"We're too close to be that formal," I said. "We can do it together. I'll wash, you dry, okay?"

"All right," she said reluctantly, and as I filled the sink with soapy water, she took a shaky breath and began scraping plates into the chicken feed bucket. "I just... I'm so mad that things like this still affect me," she said as she slid a plate into the sink.

"It's to be expected," I told her. "And you're not the only one who freaks out at noises in the night. That's part of the reason I haven't taught Chuck not to bark at strangers, even though it's annoying when I have someone out to fix the washing machine."

She shot me a grateful look as she scraped another plate. "I guess you're right. But to be honest, that's part of the reason I agreed to move in with Peter. I sleep better knowing he's next to me. It's frustrating. I just want to be okay being on my own."

"You *are* okay being on your own," I reminded her. "You've lived alone since I met you. But it's okay to spend time with someone who enriches your life and makes you feel safe; I think that's what good relationships are for."

"I guess," she said. "It just feels... weak, somehow."

"It's not," I reassured her. "We're tribal animals, after all... we're not supposed to live alone."

"But you do," she said, voicing the thought that had bubbled up in my mind as I spoke.

"I know," I said, rinsing a plate and putting it in the dish drainer. "With you and Peter moving in, and Flora and Gus breaking it off, I've been thinking about that a lot lately. I just... I think I'm afraid if we move in together, what we have just won't work as well anymore."

"Why do you think that?"

"That happened to me once before," I said.

"Really?" She dried the plate I'd just washed. "You never told me about that."

I sighed. "I was young, probably my early 20s. I'd been seeing this guy for about six months, and my roommate bailed on me. We figured it would be a good way to cut costs, since we were at each other's places all the time anyway, but once he moved in..."

"What happened?"

"I just ended up doing everything," I said, holding up the soapy bowl in my hand. "Dishes. Laundry. Cleaning. He couldn't seem to keep a job, and didn't bother to pay his share of the rent." I grimaced. "I practically went broke trying to pay the bills. It was a nightmare."

She slid a handful of spoons into the soapy water and asked, "How long did this go on for?"

"Until the lease was up, I'm sad to say. I put up with it for almost a year. I guess I was too chicken to stand up for myself."

"Hmm," she said. "That was a long time ago. And Tobias is not exactly a loafer on the job front."

"I know," I said. "It's... irrational, I suppose. But I can't seem to get past it."

"Have you two talked about it at all?"

"Not directly, no," I said. "But we're going to have to

discuss it at some point. We've been together a few years, now."

"Maybe it won't come up," Quinn said. "But I still think just because you had one bad experience with a freeloader doesn't mean every guy is like that."

"How are you two figuring out the finances, if you don't mind my asking?"

"He told me I didn't have to pay anything, but I told him I'm not living here without pulling my weight. We figured out what feels like a fair deal, and I'll give him a check the first of every month."

"And you're keeping your finances separate."

"For the foreseeable future, yes," she said. "I want to baby-step. When I was with Jed, he controlled everything... finances included. I told myself I'd never do that again."

I glanced at my friend. "So you do understand, in a way."

"It's not quite the same, but I understand why you'd want to keep your independence," she said. "Anyway, Peter and I decided we'd try it for six months and then decide if we want to keep going, or if it was better when we each had our own place."

I handed her a plate to dry. "That's so adult!"

"I know, right?" she said, grinning. "I don't know how I'll feel in six months, but I've got to tell you, right now, I'm really enjoying being here. We don't spend every moment together—he's always out working on the land, and I'm on the square most of the day—but I love coming home to him. And it's been nice to share the housework with someone." She grinned at me. "Especially since he's a little tidier than I am by nature."

I laughed. "I can see how that would be a bonus."

"I know you haven't talked about it," she said as I handed her a glass to dry, "but think about it. Tobias sounds like a completely different kind of person from the guy who free-loaded all those years ago."

"Maybe I'll just watch you and Peter and see how you get on," I said.

"Nothing wrong with that," she said, and sighed. "These old wounds we have... they can really mess with us, can't they? I just keep thinking about Flora, and what a mistake she's making."

"I feel the same way about Flora," I said. "I tried talking to her about Gus, but she seems to have made up her mind. Maybe you'll have better luck."

"I doubt it," she said, "but I'm willing to try."

We finished up the dishes together, and I was wiping down the counters when Tobias and Peter came back in.

"How are the chickens?" Quinn asked.

"They're upset," Peter said, "but we locked them down pretty well. I padlocked the gates to the goats, too... not that someone couldn't cut through the wire, but at least it'll make it more of an effort, and hopefully Pip will let us know there's a problem in time."

"Have there been goatnappings, too?" I asked.

"Not that I know of," he said, "but I don't want to risk losing anyone else."

"I should probably do the same thing at my place," I said, suddenly anxious to get back and check on my own little animal community. "Maybe I can talk to Opal tomorrow and see if anyone's following up on the license plate info."

"I think Opal's probably our best bet," Quinn said. "Lord knows Rooster isn't going to be too excited about helping Peter and me."

"The sheriff's still carrying a torch for you, eh?" Peter asked.

"Even though it's been years and years since I turned him down, he still hasn't forgiven me," Quinn said. "But I have absolutely no regrets."

"Well, I can't blame him," Peter said, wrapping his arms around my friend. "You're a catch."

Quinn smiled and turned almost as red as her hair. "You're going to give me a big head with all these nice things you keep saying."

"You deserve all of them," I reassured her. "Anyway, we should probably head out and let you guys get some sleep."

"Let's finish our whiskey first, at least," Peter protested.

"Sure," I said. "But I'm driving!"

DESPITE THE LATE NIGHT, I woke up just as the sun began to illuminate the lace curtains in my bedroom window. Tobias was asleep beside me, his long dark lashes fluttering as he dreamed. I watched my handsome boyfriend for a minute, thinking about my conversation with Quinn the night before. Was my reluctance to talk about moving in together just a response to an earlier bad experience? Or was it really that I wasn't ready yet—or maybe not ever?

Tobias must have sensed me watching him, because a moment later, his blue eyes opened. He smiled when he saw me, adorable crow's feet crinkling at the corners of his eyes. "Hey, beautiful," he said, then pulled me into him. "I love waking up next to you."

"So do I," I said. And it was true. In fact, I did sleep better with Tobias at the farmhouse—because of the animals I cared for, we almost always stayed at Dewberry Farm, instead of Tobias's little house.

We were quiet for a moment, and then Tobias said, "I can tell you're thinking about something. What is it?"

"Oh, just the whole situation with Jo," I said, not ready to bring up the subject of cohabitation just yet. "And the chickens. I need to call Opal and see if she can come up with something for me. I just don't understand why someone's stealing chickens!"

"Egg prices are up," he said, then grinned. "Maybe it's someone who owns a breakfast restaurant, and doesn't want to raise the price of omelets."

"Or chicken and waffles," I said, grimacing; I didn't like to think of what might already have happened to my little flock.

"Let's not think about that just yet," he said. "Talk to Opal; she may be able to track down that license plate today, and we might have everyone safe and sound by tonight."

"I hope you're right," I said. "But that still leaves the thing with Jo." I thought of the conversation I hadn't had yet with Alfie... and what that could mean for my friend and her family.

Tobias levered himself onto one elbow and gave me a piercing glance. "Something's bothering you. What is it?"

"Just... something I haven't told anyone about."

"Regarding what happened in the Ulrich house?"

I nodded. "I think I saw Alfie there the night Jo died."

"Why haven't you told anyone?"

"Because it involves someone I care about," I said. "If I say something to the police, it could make Alfie a suspect, but I can't believe he'd do something like that."

"This is serious," he said. "I know you care for Alfie and Molly, but not saying anything about seeing him here that night... that could be construed as obstruction. I don't need to tell you that could put you in serious trouble, too."

"I told Rooster a truck was here that night," I said. "And you know how Rooster is... if I mention Alfie's name, I want to be sure."

"You need to talk with Alfie," Tobias advised me. "And then talk to the sheriff's office."

"I know," I said. "But how do I even broach the topic?"

"Ask him point blank," Tobias said. "And ask him if he's had contact with her since she left Buttercup." He touched my face with his hand. "Sweetheart, you know what you have to do. You just don't want to."

"Can you blame me?" I asked.

"No," he said, "but you'll feel better when you've done it." He nodded toward the phone. "Why don't you text him and ask him to coffee later?"

"Today?"

"Best to get it over with," Tobias said.

I sighed and reached for the phone, texting Alfie an invitation for coffee later that day.

"What's up?" he texted back almost immediately.

"We'll talk over coffee," I replied. "Two o'clock at Bean Barn work?"

There was a long pause, during which the three dots hung for what seemed like forever. Finally, I read the words, "What is this about?"

"See you at two," I replied, and then put the phone down.

15

"Well done," Tobias said, giving me a kiss on the forehead. "I'll text the office and tell them I'm taking a late lunch. And now, mademoiselle, can I make you breakfast?"

"I only have three eggs," I reminded him. "I'm down a flock of chickens, and between the heat and the stress of losing her flock, Penny isn't laying much."

"You're only down a flock for now," he said, ever the optimist. "In the meantime, I'll figure something out. But first... coffee." He gave me another kiss and said, "Wait here," then disappeared through the doorway and walked toward the kitchen. Chuck, figuring out where he was going, waddled down the steps from the bed and followed him, his toenails clicking. The cats, on the other hand, just moved into the warm spot he'd left and curled up together.

Maybe in my next life I'd come back as a cat, I thought as I reached out and petted the purring, warm bodies. There weren't any uncomfortable conversations if you were a cat, after all.

Tobias was as good as his word; despite the dearth of eggs, he pulled together an omelet with fresh cheese, links of sausage I'd bought from the farmers' market the week before, buttered toast with jam, and two big lattes for us to share.

By the time he rolled down the driveway toward work and I was heading out to milk the goats, I was starting to think maybe living with my boyfriend full-time wasn't such a bad idea… particularly since he'd insisted on doing the dishes, too.

As I closed the front door of the farmhouse behind me and waved at Tobias's truck, my eyes flitted to the Ulrich house, and I suddenly remembered the conversation I had scheduled for later that day. My stomach tightened as I headed toward the milking parlor. Why had I agreed to this?

In truth, though, I knew I hadn't had any other choice. I set my thoughts on my work as best I could, but my mind kept floating back to Alfie.

I'd finished milking the goats and was moving irrigation hoses when my phone rang; it was Quinn.

"Any word from Opal yet?" she asked.

"Shoot… I forgot to call," I said. I'd been so distracted by the thought of my coffee I hadn't remembered I'd promised to get in touch with her. "I'll call her right now and get back to you."

"Thanks," she said. "I'm worried sick!"

"I know," I said. I hung up a moment later and dialed Opal's cell number. As the phone rang, I pulled a hose and nestled it against the roots of my rather sad-looking tomatoes. Opal answered on the fifth ring.

"Hey, Lucy! What can I do you for?"

"How did you know?" I asked. "There was another chickennapping last night," I told her.

"Another one? Dadgum it... who did they hit this time?"

"Peter Swensen over at Green Haven," I told her. "He called it in last night, and they were going to send someone over this morning, but I promised Quinn I'd call and talk to you directly. We got a partial plate number, and I know the chickennapper drives a Ford pick-up with a big cage in the back."

"All right," she said. "I've got a pen ready. What are the numbers?"

"I'm going to put you on speaker for a moment," I said. A moment later, I read off the numbers from my Notes app.

"Got it," she said. "I'll run those right now and see if we come up with anything in the area. Anything else you noticed? Did you see whoever did it?"

"I did, but it was hard to tell much about them," I confessed. "It was dark, they were wearing dark clothes..."

"Man, or woman?"

"I don't know," I said. "I wish I did."

"Well, this should give us something to go on, anyway," she said.

"Any others on the radar?"

"Just the ones you know about," Opal told me. "But I've got some news on the Ulrich House situation," she told me, lowering her voice.

"What?"

"I'm not supposed to say anything," she told me, "but the coroner's report came back, and she suffocated to death."

"I thought so," I said. "So, foul play for sure."

"That's what the report says."

"Anything else?"

"They found a few hairs they're testing for DNA," she

said. "In the meantime, Rooster plans to go down and put pressure on Rosita today. She and Ernesto have a big, dark dually, and since you reported seeing one..."

"That doesn't explain the wine glasses, though, "I said.

"I know," she said. "That's what I said to Rooster, but you know when he's got an idea, he's hard to, well, you know, influence."

"When is he going to talk to her?"

"Later on today."

"Is he going to arrest her?"

"I told him to wait on the DNA report, but you know Rooster..."

"I do," I said, feeling my heart sink.

"Anyhow, I did take the liberty of looking up that old case. You know, the Karbach accident?"

"The shooting incident? What did you find?"

"Again, you can't breathe a word to Rooster, but I pulled the incident report. Apparently the shooting wasn't the only thing that happened."

"No?"

"There were a lot of accidents out at the Karbach place. There was a fire at his place a month earlier that looked a lot like it could have been arson, and someone broke into the place just a week before he was shot."

"So someone had it in for him... or his family. Any suspects?"

"It was never followed up," she said with a snort. "Typical."

"You were here around then," I said. "Any idea who might have done it?"

"I know Alice's husband was madder than a wet hen after he found his wife between the sheets with Jimmy," she said. "But that's the only one I know about."

"I hear Alice's daughter made Jody Karbach's life at school really rough."

"I wouldn't doubt it," Opal said. "Alice was always the unofficial social code enforcer, and her daughter picked up where she left off. Bitsy was on the PTA a while back, and for a couple of months I thought we might have a murder investigation down at the high school."

"Why?"

"Bitsy wanted half the books in the library banned, and Alice just about had the school librarian fired. If Buttercup had a morality police, Bitsy'd be first in line to be sheriff. Oops! Rooster just drove up. Gotta go!"

"Thanks for the intel, Opal."

"Anytime. I hope you have better luck than Rooster figgerin' things out!"

THE NEXT THING I had to deal with, unfortunately, was a conversation with Alfie Kramer. I was about to head over toward LaGrange—I'd picked a coffee shop outside of Buttercup so that there would be fewer prying ears—when my phone rang. It was Molly.

I hesitated, then decided to let it go to voicemail, feeling a pang of guilt. Had Alfie told her about our meeting?

I watched for a voicemail to appear, but Molly didn't leave a message. Tossing the phone into my purse, I bent down to give Chuck an ear rub and headed out the front door, dreading the meeting I was about to have.

The drive to LaGrange seemed to go by in mere minutes, and my heart rose to my throat when I spotted Alfie's dually parked in the corner of the lot. I took a deep breath as I closed my own truck door behind me and headed into the coffee shop.

Alfie was alone in a corner booth, a furrow of worry between his brows. “Thanks for meeting me,” I told him. “I’m just going to get an iced green tea. Can I get you anything?” I asked.

“I’ve got a coffee coming,” he said.

I ordered from a bright, pink-cheeked barista with a ring in her nose and two studs above her left eyebrow. She made my tea and Alfie’s coffee while I waited, and a moment later I walked over to the table with both drinks.

“Here you go,” I said, pushing the coffee over to him.

“Thanks,” he said, and then, without preamble, said, “What’s this about?”

16

"You know that I know who Jo Nesbit is... or was," I said, watching his face. He blinked quickly, twice, and I continued. "And that you went to high school with her, and her original name is Jody Karbach."

I stopped and waited for him to say something, but he just looked down at his coffee cup.

"I saw you at the Ulrich House the night she died," I told him.

He looked up quickly. "Did you tell anyone else?" His voice was low and urgent, and my stomach sank even lower.

"Tobias knows," I told him, "but I haven't said anything to anyone else. I wanted to talk to you first."

He grimaced. "I'm an idiot," he said. "I wish I'd never opened that text message from her in the first place."

"What happened?" I asked in a quiet voice.

He sighed. "All right. I was hopin' this would all blow over and no one would find out I was there. But I promise you," he said, looking at me, "I didn't have anything to do with whatever happened to her that night."

"What *did* happen, then? While you were there?" I sipped my tea. "And why *were* you there?"

He let out another long, heavy sigh, and his broad shoulders drooped. "No one's gonna believe me, I'm afraid. Even if I don't go to jail, now that I've lied to Molly..."

I waited, taking a sip of my tea.

"All right," he said, looking me straight in the eye. "I'll tell you everything."

I nodded, and he took a swig from his coffee, looking like he wished it was a beer.

"Jody—well, you know that she and I knew each other in high school. She moved here in ninth grade, and I was nice to her in the cafeteria one day—Roger Murdaugh was pickin' on her, and I told him to lay off—and she kind of took a fancy to me." He took another sip of his coffee. "I already had my eye on Molly, and although I thought Jody was nice—a little weird, maybe, but nice—I didn't have any interest in her. But she kind of got... well, stalkery."

"How so?"

"Leavin' notes in my locker. And I'd catch her lookin' at me all the time. It was kinda uncomfortable, really."

"Did she actually stalk you?"

He sighed. "Well, she snuck outside my house at night and peeked through my window," he said, blushing a little bit. "My dad chased her off the property and told her to never come back, but that didn't stop her from leaving notes in my locker. She did it till the end, a few times a week."

"What did Molly think?"

"I didn't tell Molly about the notes—I just threw them out—but I think she felt bad for Jody," Alfie said. "We both did. I told Jody one day after school that I was with Molly and that I wasn't interested in her in that way, but she never gave up. And then her dad died in that huntin' blind, and

Bitsy and her cheerleader friends were just so mean to her..."

"I heard about that. The sheriff thought it was an accident, apparently."

"Uh huh." He rolled his eyes. "Shot in a deer blind outside of huntin' season. I think everyone in town knew it was no accident, but the Karbachs weren't from around here, and Jimmy had stirred up a lot of trouble, so..." He shrugged. "Nothin' ever came of it."

"What kind of trouble did he stir up?"

"The man was a hound dog. And he managed to get Alice Green, Bitsy's mama, into bed. It would've been okay if her husband hadn't come home early from work and found them under the covers. I always wondered if maybe it wasn't Fred Green who was responsible for that hunting accident. Word is he was out of town when it happened, but still..."

"Why do you think that?"

"He was furious," Alfie said. "Word is he wouldn't talk to her for more than six months. Things were rough in the Green household for a long time. And things got harder for Jody, even though she had nothin' to do with her daddy's choices."

"So the town turned on Jody?"

"Mostly Bitsy," he said. "She had a lot of power; she was a popular cheerleader. I think she dealt with whatever shame she had over her mama by takin' it out on poor Jody."

"Did Jody graduate?"

He shook his head. "If she did, she didn't do it here. She left halfway through senior year. Her dad was gone by then, so she was on her own."

"Where did she go?"

He shrugged. "Nobody knew, and nobody paid much attention. We all figured she'd gone to live with family somewhere. I guess she managed to make good." He shook his head. "It's a shame she came back."

"Why *did* she come back?" I asked.

"I think... I think she was tryin' to even the score. Make life hard for the folks who made hers hard, all those years ago."

"And why did you agree to go see her?"

Alfie darted a wary glance at me. "She told me she had some information she needed to share with me. About—about someone important to me." He took a deep breath. "And that if I didn't come to visit, she'd go to the police with it."

"What did she know?"

"That's the thing," he said. "She never told me all of it. I don't know if she really had something, or if she was just using it as a way to get me to visit her."

"Why didn't she?"

Alfie flushed. "Because the moment I walked in the door, she tried to get me to drink a glass of wine. I said no a thousand times before she gave up, just poured one for herself and drank half of it down right there."

He was quiet, and his face flushed. I knew this was hard for him. He took a deep breath before he continued. "Then... then she grabbed hold of me and pulled me over to the couch and told me to sit down, and then she started unbuttoning her blouse and tryin' to sit on my lap. Kept tellin' me if I just stayed a little longer... and then she started touching me." He shuddered. "I told her I'm a married man and I don't do that kind of thing, but she wouldn't take no for an answer."

"What happened?"

"I stood up and told her if she had something to share, she'd better share it. Because I was leavin'."

"And?"

"She looked... well, she looked hurt, at least for a moment. Like the girl I remembered in high school, all sad and lost." He took a deep breath. "Then she got this smile on her face. It was a knowing smile, like she really did have somethin' to tell me, but was goin' to hold onto it unless I changed my mind. 'You'll be back,' she said, and I walked out of that house, got in my truck and headed straight home. I've been kickin' myself ever since." He put his elbows on the table and his head in his hands. "And now she's dead, and I'm the last person who saw her alive, and my wife doesn't know I was there, and if I tell her she's gonna know I lied to her and Rooster's gonna think I'm the one who killed her."

I turned my cup around on the table a few times, wishing I had an answer he would like.

"We've always been honest with each other," he said in a hoarse voice. "If I tell her about this now... I'm afraid she'll never forgive me."

"Will you be able to forgive yourself if you don't?"

"No," he said, his voice raw. "I won't. This'll tear us apart either way, I know that." He looked up at me. "But if Rooster decides I'm the one who did... whatever someone did to her, and I end up in jail, I won't be there for my kids. I won't be there for Molly." His voice cracked, and his eyes were red. "Lucy. Help me find out what happened that night. I know I didn't lay a finger on that woman, but if we don't find out who did..."

"I'll do everything I can to help," I said. "But I think you have to tell Molly what you just told me."

He seemed to deflate a little bit, his face crumpling. "I don't think she'll ever be able to trust me again."

"You've been together a long time. You've always been a

straight shooter, and I believe what you told me," I said. "But I'm kind of curious why you didn't tell her you were going there in the first place."

He sighed. "I think it's because I was afraid of what Jody was gonna tell me." He was silent for a minute, then took a deep breath and seemed to make up his mind. "She said—she said she knew something about Bobby. Bobby Green, Bitsy's brother. He used to be my best friend. Even if we don't see that much of each other now, I still care about him. I wanted to find out what she had to say before I decided what to do about it."

"What about him?" I asked, thinking it was the Green family, once again. Had Bobby or his father taken revenge on Jody's father all those years ago?

"She said she had evidence that he was involved in what happened to her daddy," Alfie said. "She told me she'd only share it with me if I met with her alone... and if I didn't, she'd go to the police with it." He grimaced. "I should've just left it alone."

"What kind of evidence?"

"She didn't say," he said. "She'd only dropped those hints when we were texting, but when she was coming on to me like that I left, before she said anything more. And now I'm wonderin' if they found anything on her computer, or at the house, and I went through all of that for nothing."

"Do you think Bobby Green might have had something to do with the death of Jody's dad?"

"I don't know," he said. "He was upset about what happened with his mama, of course. But I can't see him shooting Jody's dad over it." He ran his hands through his hair. "Why did she have to come back?"

"I don't know, but she did," I said.

He looked up at me from troubled eyes. “I really have to tell Molly, don’t I?”

I nodded.

He let out another long sigh, then pushed back his chair and stood up. “Thanks for talkin’ with me, helping me figure out what to do next. It helps to tell someone... I’ve been holdin’ onto this since that night, and it’s killin’ me. I hate secrets and lies.”

“Tell Molly that,” I said. “You’ve been together long enough I’m sure she’ll understand.”

“I hope you’re right,” he said. “And I hope Rooster understands, too,” he added.

For myself, I didn’t count on it.

17

I was on my way back to Dewberry Farm, still reviewing my conversation with Alfie in my head, when my phone rang. It was Opal.

"What's up?" I asked.

"Well, I came up empty on the partial plate you gave," she said. "Are you sure you got the digits right?"

"I think so," I said, feeling deflated. Was it too late for Niblet and the rest of the girls? It had been days since they'd disappeared, and I hoped they hadn't been transformed into pot pie and served up for dinner somewhere.

"Maybe I'll try a few similar digits, just to be sure," she said.

"Thanks," I said. "Any other news?"

"Well, I did do some more diggin' on the old Karbach case."

"The 'accidental' hunting death?"

"That one, yes. Apparently one of the deputies thought it might not be accidental, and said so, but the sheriff overruled her."

"Different decade, same type of sheriff," I said. "Were

there any notes on what she thought might have happened?"

She lowered her voice. "There were two suspects," she said. "And neither one had an alibi."

"Who were they?"

"One was Fred Green," she said.

"Of course," I said. "He caught Jimmy with his wife, after all."

"He's good with a rifle, too," Opal said. "My cousin used to go huntin' with him."

"Were there any threats?" I asked.

"You mean other than when he found Jimmy in bed with his wife and threatened to geld him?"

"Oh. Wow. Yes," I said.

"None that I know of," Opal said, "but that kinda speaks for itself, don't it?"

"You're not wrong," I said. "So who's the other person?"

"His son, Bobby."

Alfie's best friend... the one Jody had told Alfie she had incriminating information about. I swallowed hard, thinking back to my conversation that afternoon. Had Alfie told me the truth? Or had Alfie told Bobby what Jody had shared... and had Bobby been responsible for both deaths?

"You still there?" Opal asked.

"Yes, I'm here," I said. "He would have been in high school at the time, though, right?"

"He was a senior at the time, as I recall," she said.

"Why was he a suspect?"

"He told Jody Karbach he was going to kill her father. Wrote it in a note and put it in her locker, actually. Along with a few foul comments about Jody."

"Ouch," I said. "And they still ruled it an accident?"

"Welcome to the Kocurek School of Law Enforcement," Opal said dryly.

"In Bobby's defense, high schoolers don't have the best judgment in terms of what they commit to paper," I said. "And the circumstances were challenging."

"Even so."

"I'm not disagreeing with you," I said. "Are you thinking what happened to Jody might be related to what happened to her father?"

"I've been thinkin' on that," she said. "I heard she was goin' after a lot of local places, tryin' to force 'em to sell. I'm wondering if maybe she let somethin' drop to someone who didn't want all this drug up again."

"I know some of the properties she was going after," I said, "but not all of them."

"I'll see what I can find out," she said. "Anything from your end?"

"Ah... not really," I said. Alfie's story was Alfie's story to tell, after all.

"Hmm," Opal said. "That sounds like more than nothing."

"I'm... following up on something," I said. "I'll let you know if it pans out."

"You better not be holdin' out on me," she said.

"Of course not," I reassured her. "Let me know if you find anything else out about the properties Jody was going after, okay?"

"I will," she said. "Oh, I gotta go, Rooster's coming."

I hung up a moment later, disturbed by what Alfie had told me. Was Jody killed because she stirred up something about a murder that had happened decades ago? Had Alfie really left that night without finding out what she claimed to have on his friend Bobby Green?

Or was there something I was missing altogether?

When I got home, I pulled out my creaky laptop and typed in Bobby Green's name. A familiar face popped up; I recognized him from around town, although I hadn't realized he was friends with Alfie.

His Facebook profile showed a picture of him with a pretty, red-haired woman and two tow-headed children. I browsed through his public albums; evidently he was an avid hunter, as there were several photos of recently deceased bucks. In one of them, he was next to a blonde woman in a pink-and-green camo shirt with a smile so perfect it looked like she might have shelled out for veneers. Although she'd changed her last name when she married, I recognized her as Bitsy, his sister. In front of them lay a dead buck. I scrolled through the rest of the photos, some of which showed Bobby's parents, whose marriage had somehow survived the matriarch's early indiscretion, at what appeared to be Christmas and anniversary dinners. Neither of Bobby's parents had profiles, but his sister Bitsy did. I clicked on her name and was led to her page. Apparently she was a real estate agent based out of LaGrange, and most of her feed consisted of pictures of listings she'd recently acquired. I looked through her friend list, a little surprised to see Jo Nesbit listed there. I clicked on Jo's page again, scrolling through her timeline, which was scant, except for announcements about acquisitions her company had made. Until her recent spree in Buttercup, most of her work seemed to have centered around the Dallas area, and consisted of what appeared to be distressed commercial buildings. Although Jo and Bitsy were Facebook friends, I saw no sign of interaction on either page.

If Bitsy hated Jo so much, why would they be Facebook friends? Unless Bitsy didn't recognize her. I remembered suddenly the real estate agent's card I'd found in the Ulrich house. It was Bitsy's. She really must not have known. But maybe her brother recognized her, after all these years.

I scrolled down and found a reference to a recent sale on Jo's Facebook page. Bitsy had handled the listing of the building that housed Rosita's restaurant. The one Jo's company had bought. So there was a current-day connection between the Green family and Jody Karbach. Had Bitsy finally figured out who she was and told her family Jody was back in town?

Or had Jody mentioned something about the Green family's involvement with the "accidental" shooting that caught her attention... and had Bobby (or his father) killed Jody to make sure she didn't have a chance to share what she knew with the police?

I wished Alfie hadn't ever gone to the Ulrich house that night. But since he had, I now wished he'd stayed long enough to find out what it was Jody knew.

18

I waited to hear from Alfie or Molly that whole afternoon, but my phone didn't ring... until Mandy called me just before five.

"He arrested my mom," she said.

"Oh, no," I said.

"Said she suffocated Jody Karbach for buying the building and trying to put the family out of business," she said, sounding miserable.

"What proof does he have?"

"I don't know," she said. "I've got to get her out of there, though. What do you have?"

"I'm looking into the Green family," I said. "I just don't have anything concrete yet."

"Any other options?"

"None that have come up," I said, dismissing the thought that floated up to the top of my head... Alfie.

"We've got to figure this out," she said.

"I'm going to head over to talk to Bitsy Hauser right now," I said.

"I'll come with you."

"No," I said. "I think it's better if I go. I can tell her I'm thinking of listing the farm, now that property prices are up. And then I'll mention the Ulrich house and see what she does."

"Are you sure?"

"I am," I said. "I'll let you know how it goes!"

IT WAS ALMOST six o'clock when I pulled into the parking lot by Bitsy's office. Our former Buttercup real estate agent, Faith Zapalac, had put her home base right by the square, but Bitsy's office was located in an old brick building that looked like it might have enjoyed a previous life as an auto parts store, halfway between Buttercup and LaGrange.

I parked next to a black Cadillac Escalade (what was it with realtors and Escalades?), pushed open the plate glass door of the office, and walked in. A young man in a button-down shirt and glasses looked up at me with a professional smile. "Can I help you?"

"Yes," I said. "Is Bitsy here?"

"You got here just in time," he said. "She hasn't left yet. Do you have an appointment?"

"No," I said. "Does she have a few minutes to talk to me about maybe listing a property?"

That, evidently, was the right thing to say. "I'm sure she'll have time for that. I'll get her," he said, and disappeared down a fluorescent-lit hallway as I sat down on one of the maroon chairs in the waiting room. A picture of Buttercup's square adorned one of the white walls, along with several plaques celebrating "agents of the year." Bitsy had won two of them.

A few moments later, Bitsy appeared in a cloud of floral

perfume, looking every bit the mature former cheerleader. She wore a form-fitting fuchsia dress that plunged to reveal a tasteful amount of cleavage. Her hair was sleek and blonde, and artfully styled around her preternaturally smooth face.

"Well hello there," she said, extending a manicured hand and smiling. "I'm Bitsy Hauser. I understand you're thinking of listing a property?"

"I'm Lucy Resnick," I said, shaking her hand. "Good to meet you. And yes, yes I am."

"Why don't you come on back?" she offered, and I followed her perfume down the hallway to an office on the right. "Can I get you a drink before we get started?"

"Seltzer if you have it," I said.

"I'll be right back," she said, and disappeared back into the hallway after gesturing me to one of the maroon chairs by the window. I sat down, glancing around the office. A neat stack of files sat on top of her glass desk, and an expensive laptop stood open. I was tempted to peek at what was on the screen, but there wasn't enough time. A moment later, she reappeared with two cans of generic lime seltzer, offering one to me and popping the top on the second one for herself. She settled herself in the other maroon armchair. "Now, then," she said, taking a delicate sip of her drink. "What kind of property do you have?"

"I've got a small farm, about ten acres," I said.

"Oooh, sounds lovely," she said. "Where is it?"

"Only a few minutes from the square, on Round Top Road."

"Is there a home on the property?"

"A farmhouse that's about a hundred years old," I said.

"Habitable?"

"Well, I'm living there," I said, grinning, "so I guess that would be a yes."

"What's the address?" she asked, getting up and sitting down at the desk behind her laptop. I reeled it off, and she pulled up the property online.

"Oooh, that's a pretty little piece of property," she said. "Is it improved at all?"

"I've got a barn, and I run a couple of cows and some goats on it; the rest is a small peach orchard and veggies."

"And you back on Dewberry Creek. That'll be a bonus," she said, looking up from her screen at me. "I think this will sell in a heartbeat, as long as you price it right. Unfortunately, with mortgage rates skyrocketing right now, we have to be conservative with pricing to ensure a sale."

"Of course," I said.

"How did you find out about me, if you don't mind my asking?"

"Someone I know recommended you," I said. "I heard you recently sold the Rosita's building for a good price."

She blinked quickly. "Yes," she said. "The seller was very happy with the offer."

"Who bought it, anyway? I heard it was someone from out of town?"

"The buyer was a company from Dallas," she said.

"Yes, it was their representative that recommended you," I said. "Jo Nesbit."

She blinked again, and swallowed. "Jo Nesbit? I'm not sure I know her."

"Oh, I'm sure you do," I said. "She said wonderful things about how efficient you were. That she was looking at your other listings, too... apparently she was planning to invest heavily in Buttercup before... well, you know."

"I know what?" Her voice was clipped.

"Didn't you hear? She died," I said.

"I didn't know," she said, eyes darting to the window. "I'm very sorry to hear that. Anyway..."

"I heard a rumor about her, actually, just earlier today. That she used to go to school here in Buttercup, only she was called something else. Jody Karbach."

Her voice turned cold. "I'm sorry... but are you here to list your property, or did you have something else in mind?"

"Oh, I want to list," I said. "I just like to get to know people when I'm working with them. And of course I'm curious if you know anything about Jo... Jody."

"No," she said. "I'm afraid that name isn't familiar to me."

"Are you sure?" I asked. "I heard that there was some... well, bad blood between your family and the Karbachs back in the day. Before Jimmy Karbach died."

She snapped her laptop closed and stood up. "I'm afraid I have another appointment to go to. If you'd like to list, please let me know and I can come out and view the property and provide you a listing estimate." She plucked a business card from a plexiglass box on her desk. "Now, if you'll excuse me, I really must be going."

I blinked innocently. "Did I say something to offend you?"

"Of course not," she said, with a smile that didn't reach her eyes. "I just realized what time it is, and I don't want to be late for my client. Now, I'll have Colin take down your details, and someone will give you a follow-up call in the next day or two." She shepherded me toward her office door, turning to lock it behind her once we were through, and then down the hallway toward the front door.

She addressed the young man behind the desk. "I told Ms... Resnick, was it?"

"Yes," I said. "Lucy Resnick."

"I told Ms. Resnick that you'll take down her details and that someone will follow up with her. I have a showing I just realized I'm almost late to."

"I thought they canceled," Colin said, looking confused.

"It's back on," she said, and turned to me. "Nice to meet you. Colin will be able to help you with anything you need. Have a good day!"

And with that, she was gone.

"Well, that was kind of odd," I said.

"Oh, she's a busy lady," Colin said, but didn't look convinced.

"How long have you been with the company?" I asked.

"I started about six months ago. I'm learning the ropes; I'll be taking my exam to get my license in a few weeks."

"Do you know Bitsy well?"

"She's the best," he said. "I'm sorry she rushed off like that... she is really the most organized agent we have."

"Oh, I think I must have upset her."

"Upset her? How?"

"Do you know anything about Jo Nesbit?"

"Doesn't ring a bell," he said.

"She's the buyer for the building Rosita's is in," I prompted him.

"Oh. Oh, yes. We double-ended that deal, actually. She was represented by someone else in the agency. Unfortunately, I don't think it closed... with what happened to Ms. Nesbit."

"Really?"

"We're seeing what we can do, but it looks like it might not go through."

"If Jo was represented by another agent, does that mean she was in the office?"

He nodded. "She was."

"Did Bitsy meet her at all?"

"Not that I saw. Anyway, let me get your info, and I'll follow up with you tomorrow to see if we can set up a time?"

"Sure," I said, and gave him my name and number. "Thanks for fitting me in today."

"Of course," he said. "I hope we'll be working with you soon!"

Molly's car was in the driveway when I pulled up to Dewberry Farm about fifteen minutes later. My heart squeezed as I closed my truck door behind me and walked up to the front porch, where she sat in one of my rocking chairs, hugging herself.

"He lied to me," she said, and burst into tears.

19

"Oh, sweetheart," I said, opening my arms. She hurtled into them, and I held her for a long moment as she sobbed into my chest. "Come inside where it's cool and tell me all about it," I said finally. She pulled away and swiped at her eyes.

"Okay," she said in a very small voice and followed me into the farmhouse.

I sat her down at my grandmother's table and poured her a big glass of iced tea and one for myself, then sat down next to her.

"Tell me what happened," I said.

"You know already," she said bitterly. "Why didn't you tell me?"

"When I figured it out, I wanted to give him the chance to tell you," I said. "He was beside himself."

She looked up at me, eyes red and swollen. "He said he didn't touch her. That it was innocent. Do you believe him?"

"I do," I confessed. "I think he was trying to protect his friend."

"Bobby Green?" She scoffed. "Alfie's been a better friend

to him than he has been to Alfie. What did he think she knew?"

"Something about the death of Jody Karbach's father, I think. I think Alfie thought she had some sort of incriminating information about him. Didn't he tell you?"

"I didn't give him a chance," she said. "As soon as he told me he was there that night, I grabbed my keys and ran out the door. I... I couldn't even look at him, much less listen to any explanation." She gave a loud sniffle, and I reached for a tissue and handed it to her. "What kind of incriminating information?"

"I think it's about the death of Jimmy Karbach all those years ago."

"That was an accident," she said.

"That's what it was ruled at the time," I said. "But Mandy Vargas and Opal both agree that it was suspicious."

"Like Rooster's gonna reopen a case that closed more than twenty years ago," Molly said. "I don't think I buy it."

"Why else would he come here? From what I hear, she had a crush on him in high school, but it was never mutual."

"Have you seen her now? She's hot. Or at least she was. And I've just kind of gone south these past few years, after four kids... I'm not that cute girl he fell for in high school."

I blinked; I knew Molly felt self-conscious about her looks, but hadn't realized it had gone this far. "I don't think he had any interest in Jody Karbach, Molly. I think he was trying to protect his friend, and then when Jody turned up dead, he panicked."

"He wasn't going to tell me he went there in the first place," she said. "We're not supposed to have secrets. What else is he hiding from me?"

I reached out to touch her arm. "I don't think he is, if I'm being honest. I think he just made a bad decision and couldn't see a way out of it."

Her face hardened. "Whose side are you on, anyway? I thought you were my friend."

"I am," I said. "And I totally understand why you're upset."

"Do you? It doesn't sound like it," she said. "I have to go. I have to get out of here. I have to think."

"Molly..."

"No, Lucy. I don't want to be talked into how to feel. I need to sort this out on my own." With that, my friend shoved back her chair and stumbled toward the front door. I followed, wishing I knew what to say, and watched as she jerked her Dodge Caravan into reverse and hurtled down the driveway, leaving a cloud of dust in her wake.

Had I interfered too much? Had I overstepped my bounds?

I returned to the kitchen and picked up Chuck, hugging him to me as I wondered what I could have done differently... and if I'd lost one of my dearest friends.

I WAS STILL TORN up about Molly as I worked through my chores that evening. I'd called Tobias to talk, but it was surgery day at the clinic and he didn't answer, so I left a message asking him to call me back and headed outside to work off my anxiety.

Even though the sun was setting, it was still close to 100 degrees, and I was sweating through my Buttercup Market Days T-shirt as I turned on the irrigation hoses for my tomatoes and spinach, finished refilling the goats' water, and checked on poor, lonely Penny. I wasn't ready to give up on my missing chickens yet, but if I didn't find them soon, I was going to have to invest in some new chicks.

After finishing my chores with the evening milking, I picked a few ripe tomatoes and headed inside to figure out dinner.

I was going to make a quick and easy grilled cheese sandwich, but the red ripe tomatoes in my hand gave me a different idea. I pulled out my grandmother's cookbook and leafed through to one of my favorite of her summertime recipes: tomato pie.

After a quick survey of the fridge to make sure I had the requisite ingredients, I pulled a pie crust from the freezer and preheated the oven. (I usually tried to avoid turning on the oven this time of year, but I knew a warm slice of tomato pie would be worth the extra heat.)

As the oven preheated, I sliced the tomatoes and put them in a colander in the sink, sprinkling them with salt to help drain the extra juice.

My mind kept turning to Molly and Alfie as I measured sour cream and mayonnaise into a bowl, then added grated cheese, salt, and pepper into the creamy mixture. Did Molly believe that something had happened between Alfie and Jo? Had something happened?

And was I wrong in believing Alfie was innocent of what happened to Jo?

As I layered pie weights on the crust before popping it into the oven to brown, I wondered if everything Alfie had told me was true. He'd said that Jody told him she had information that would incriminate Bobby. But if that was true, why call Alfie, and not Bobby, if blackmail was what she had in mind?

Then again, blackmail might not have been what Jo was interested in. She had seemed to have plenty of money.

What she didn't have was Alfie... and if she'd been carrying a torch all those years, her whole goal might have been to kindle a new romance with her old crush. That was what Alfie had reported, anyway.

What information had she had? And had Alfie told me the whole truth about what had happened?

As much as I hated to admit it, I had a niggling fear that maybe more had happened in the Ulrich house than Alfie had let on.

When the pie crust was done, I pulled it from the oven, removed the weights, and layered the drained tomatoes over the crust. Then I spread the cheesy mixture over the tomatoes and slid the pie into the oven, setting the timer and anticipating the delicious smell that would soon be wafting through the kitchen.

As I washed the dishes, the phone rang. I picked it up and Tobias greeted me.

"Sorry I missed your call earlier," he said.

"No worries... I knew it was a surgery day."

"What's up?" he asked.

I told him about my day, and he groaned. "Wow. Sounds like you could use a hug."

"I could, actually. What are you up to this evening?"

"I was hoping to see you, actually," he said.

"Well, I just put a tomato pie in the oven," I told him. "It'll be ready in just under a half hour."

"The tomato pie from your grandmother's cookbook? The cheesy one with the crust that melts in your mouth?"

I laughed, already feeling better. "Come join me," I said.

"I have a cold bottle of white wine in the fridge... I'll bring it."

"That would be awesome," I said. "See you soon."

I hung up, feeling much better just knowing Tobias

would be over soon, and opened the fridge again, wondering what to do for dessert. I was out of fresh fruit... but the oven was already on and I did have some frozen dewberries left. I pulled out the bag of frozen berries and opened my grandmother's cookbook to her Dewberry Pie Bars. It took only a few minutes to assemble the delicious brown sugar shortbread crust. After whisking the dry ingredients together, I combined melted butter, white and brown sugar, vanilla, and lemon zest, then folded the wet and dry ingredients together. I pressed the dough into a parchment-lined baking pan and slid it into the oven below the pie, reserving some dough for the topping, then measured out berries into a saucepan along with sugar, salt, cornstarch, and some lemon zest and lemon juice. By the time the mixture was bubbling, the crust was ready; I pulled it out of the oven, spooned the dewberry mixture over it, crumbled the remaining dough over the top and popped it into the oven just before the timer went off for the pie.

By the time Tobias arrived, the pie had cooled enough to eat and the dewberry pie bars were filling the kitchen with a sweet, lemon-vanilla scent.

"It smells incredible in here," Tobias said after kissing me hello.

"I used up most of the rest of my dewberries for dessert," I said. "The oven was already on, so I decided to make the most of it."

"A glass of chilled wine will help cool us off," Tobias said, pulling a corkscrew out of the drawer by the oven and opening the bottle he'd brought.

"If you'll take care of that, I'll put some fresh basil on the pie and get a salad together."

"I got the easy end of the bargain," he said. "I'll do dishes."

"Deal," I said. As he filled our glasses, I pulled together a salad, dressed it simply with white vinegar, garlic salt, olive oil and a bit of crumbled goat cheese, and a few minutes later we were toasting each other over gooey slices of warm tomato pie.

"I'm sorry you had such a rough day," he said, reaching to squeeze my hand before digging into his pie.

"Thanks," I said. "It helps having you here. It would have been hard to be by myself tonight."

He paused with a forkful of pie. "I've been thinking about that, actually," he said.

I swallowed and focused on cutting into my own slice of pie. "Oh?"

"I like having you around," he said. "With Peter and Quinn moving in together, it got me thinking... maybe we should talk a little bit about where we see our future going."

"That makes sense," I said. "I love having you in my life. I know we spend more time here than at your place, and sometimes I feel bad about it, but with everything I have to take care of here..."

"Are you thinking we try living together at Dewberry Farm?" he asked.

"It's something to consider," I said.

"You don't think your grandmother would disapprove?" he asked.

As he spoke, a cool breeze wafted through the room, and despite the heat outside and the warmth from the oven, I shivered. "Do you smell that?"

"Lavender," he said.

"My grandmother's scent," I said. "Since we're having two of her favorite recipes tonight, I guess it's appropriate."

"So, is that a warning?" he asked. "Or a blessing?"

The smell of lavender grew stronger, and a feeling of

love flowed through me... it was almost as if I could feel my grandmother's arms around me.

"A blessing," I said, just as the timer went off on the oven. "Sorry... bad timing," I said. "Be right back... I just have to take the bars out."

As I set the golden brown dewberry pie bars down on top of the stove and reached to turn off the oven, the lights flickered, and there was another cool breeze.

Danger. I wasn't sure if I heard the word or it was just a feeling, but suddenly, my skin crawled.

"What was that?" Tobias asked.

"I don't know," I said, "but there's something wrong."

As I spoke, the lights went out again. I turned away from the oven and had just taken a step when Chuck growled. As I took another step, he launched himself toward the front door, right in front of my feet. I tripped right over him and fell to my knees. As my palms hit the floor, shots rang out from the front of the house.

20

"Stay down!" Tobias yelled. I flattened myself to the floor, reached for Chuck, and hugged him hard, putting my body between him and the front of the house as another volley of shots sounded, along with the sound of breaking glass and splintering wood.

"Are you okay?" Tobias whispered after the second volley stopped.

"I think so," I whispered back. "You?"

"I'm fine," he said. "You have Chuck?"

"I do," I said. Chuck was trembling and growling in my arms, and it was all I could do to keep him from wriggling from my grasp and lunging at the front door. "I hope the kittens are okay," I said. "And the goats. Can we go check on them?"

"We're not going anywhere yet," he said. "We don't know if they're done."

He scooched closer to me and pulled me to him, keeping his body between me and the door. We stayed silent, listening for voices, footsteps, anything... but there was nothing. After what felt like hours, but was probably no more than two or three minutes, the lights flickered back on again.

"Stay down," Tobias said again as he got to his knees and crawled toward the front of the house. He peered through the front windows. "I can't see anyone, but it's still dark," he said. "I'm calling the police. We're staying low till they get here."

"Okay," I said, still holding Chuck as Tobias spoke with the 911 dispatcher. He stayed on the line as we waited, praying (at least I was) that a volley of shots wouldn't tear through the house a second time.

It felt like ages before the red and blue lights flashed outside, followed by the bright beams of flashlights flickering around the perimeter of the house. When Deputy Shames appeared at the door and gave us the all clear, I felt the tension I'd been holding without knowing it leach from my body, and tears leaked from my eyes.

As I climbed to my feet, still holding Chuck, Tobias enfolded the two of us in a huge hug, then stood back and looked me over. "Are you sure you're not hurt?"

"Banged up knees, but that's it," I said shakily, lowering Chuck to the floor. "The house is going to need a little bit of work, though," I said, surveying the splintered wood walls, the broken windows. "If I hadn't tripped over Chuck..." I glanced down at my apricot poodle, who was now wagging his tail and looking up at me from his soft brown eyes, then looked at the hole in the wall almost directly behind where my head had been just before the shots were fired.

"All that matters is that you're okay," Tobias reassured me. "We can fix the house a lot easier than we can fix you."

"I hate to interrupt," Deputy Shames said from the

doorway to the kitchen, "but are you both ready to give a statement?"

"We are," Tobias said. "But I'm afraid we won't be much help."

"Why not?"

"We didn't see or hear anyone coming up the driveway. All we heard were shots."

"You have no idea who might have done this?"

Tobias and I looked at each other.

"No," I said.

It was almost one in the morning by the time we managed to get the glass cleared up and the broken windows boarded over. The police had found shell casings out in front of the house, and had taken some of the bullets with them for analysis. The animals, thankfully, were all okay, and the damage was limited to the house.

Unfortunately, there was nothing to be done about the bullet holes in the walls, at least not tonight. My house felt violated, and the boards over the windows were an all-too-visible reminder of what had happened just hours ago.

Although a deputy was stationed in the driveway to make sure the attacker didn't return, I still felt unsafe.

I cut each of us a dewberry pie bar, and we sat down at the table and bit into the tangy, crunchy cookies.

"These are delicious," I said.

"They are," he said. "And we've got a whole pan of them?"

I nodded.

"I'm going to gain fifteen pounds if I take up residence here," he joked.

"Oh, never fear... I'll put you to work and you'll burn it all off," I said with a grin. There was always something to be done on the farm, after all.

He finished off the last bite and I followed suit. Then he slid the plates into the dishwasher and held out a hand. "Let's get you to bed," he said.

I took his hand and followed him to the unscathed part of the house, grateful he was with me tonight.

As we settled in under the fluffy covers a few minutes later, Chuck depositing himself at our feet and Smoky and Lucky nestled on our pillows, he reached and pulled me into his arms, burying his face in my hair.

"I'm so glad you're okay," he breathed. "Tonight, I realized if anything happened to you... I don't know what I'd do."

"I know. I feel the same way about you," I said, feeling comforted by the warmth of his arms around me. "Do you think whoever did that will be back?"

"I don't know," he said, "but I know I'm staying here at least until they get this figured out. You're too precious to risk losing."

I hugged him tight, but my mind was still buzzing... even now I hadn't seemed to be able to clear all the adrenaline from my system.

"Who do you think might have done this?" I asked. I hadn't had an answer for the police, but it was a question I'd been running over in my head all night.

"Who did you talk to today?"

"Alfie, of course," I said. "And Molly came over, and left really upset with me. But I can't imagine it would be either of them."

"Me neither," he agreed. "Who else?"

"I stopped by Bitsy Hauser's office," I told him. "Afterwards. I told her I was thinking of listing Dewberry Farm and mentioned that I'd seen she was the listing agent on the Rosita's building."

"How did she respond to that?"

"Well, I probably asked too many probing questions, but she went from having all the time in the world to needing to get to an urgent appointment within about five minutes."

"Huh. What probing questions did you ask?"

"I mentioned Jody's real name—or her original name—and asked a few things about her. And that's when Bitsy shut up like a clam."

"I'm beginning to think that whatever happened to Jody might have something to do with what happened all those years ago... the 'hunting accident'."

"I'm thinking the same thing," I said. "I'm wondering if maybe Fred Green or his son might have been responsible for the 'accidental' death of Jody's dad."

"I was thinking that, too. But if Jody had something incriminating on Bobby, why not go to the police? And why wait all these years to say something?"

"That's the thing, isn't it? It doesn't seem to make sense. I've read that sometimes trauma victims take a long time to process things and be able to confront whoever caused the trauma," I said. "It could be something like that. Or maybe she thought she'd be more likely to be listened to as a successful businesswoman than a teenager."

"But she didn't go to the police about it," Tobias pointed out.

"No," I agreed. "At least not from what Opal's said. Although maybe she said something to the police when it happened, only to have it dismissed." I thought about it for a moment. "It's always possible she didn't actually have anything incriminating. Maybe it was just a ruse to get Alfie over."

"Alfie must have had some suspicion that Bobby was involved if he was willing to go listen to her," Tobias posited. "Either that, or that wasn't the real reason he went over there."

"You're thinking Alfie lied to me?"

"I'm not thinking anything," he said. "I'm just exploring possibilities."

"Why else would he have gone over there?"

He was quiet for a moment. "Molly and Alfie have been married for a long time. Maybe he was... intrigued. Or flattered by the attention, at least."

"You think he was going to cheat on Molly?"

"I don't think or know anything," he said. "I'm just trying to come up with possibilities."

"I don't think I like your possibilities," I said.

"I don't particularly like them either," he said. "One thing I am sure of, though, is that someone is scared. And you've stirred up something that someone would rather remained uncovered."

"Tonight was a threat."

"Yes," he said. "And it may have been meant to be more than a threat. If you hadn't tripped over Chuck..."

I shivered. "I know," I said quietly. "I think it's time to go talk with Bobby Green."

"After what happened today? No way," he said.

"If you go with me?"

"Maybe," he said, sighing. "I just wish we had a competent sheriff."

"But we don't," I reminded him. "And Rosita's in jail, and somebody shot up my home."

"Fine," he said. "But you have to wait until after work. Because I am definitely coming with you."

I gave him another squeeze and put my head on his chest, thankful for a partner who—literally—had my back.

21

The next day went by slowly, and there was a lot more traffic than usual in front of the farm, as truck after truck slowed down to peer at the damage from the night before. It hadn't been a good week for me; not only was my flock missing with no progress on discovering who had stolen them, but my poor house was no longer a haven for me. I'd called the insurance company and an adjustor was coming out later in the week, and in the meantime, I was having to live with boarded-up windows... and fear.

Was the "message" enough? Or had someone tried to kill me... and would they come back and try again?

To make things worse, Molly wouldn't return my calls, and Alfie was ignoring me, too. Mandy, on the other hand, called me every thirty minutes, checking for updates, even though I'd told her I was following up on a lead and would be out of pocket. Now that her mother had been arrested, she was desperate to find at least one other suspect in the death of Jo Nesbit, though, so I couldn't blame her. I hadn't told her about Alfie's visit to the house the night Jo died, and I had no way of knowing if he had shared that information with the sheriff's office yet, so as a courtesy to the Kramers, I was saying nothing on the topic.

"But who shot up your house?" she asked.

"I don't know," I said.

"Who have you talked to lately?"

"I spoke with Bitsy Hauser yesterday," I said, "and Mary down at the Enchanted Florist before that, and Edna down at the Red & White."

"Huh. Do you think that this, and maybe what happened to Jody Karbach, could be linked with her father's death?"

"I don't know," I said again.

"Well, you're no help at all," she huffed, impatient. "Do the police have any ideas?"

"If they do, they're not sharing them with me," I said.

"Can I come out and take pictures of your house for the next edition?"

"I suppose so," I said. "I'll be here until about six."

"Where are you going then?"

"To dinner with my boyfriend," I said, more tartly than I meant to. I wanted so much to help Mandy, but there were things I did not feel it was my place to tell her, at least not yet. I knew she was frustrated with me.

My phone beeped, and I pulled it from my ear and glanced at it; it was the sheriff's office.

"I've got to go," I told Mandy. "I promise I'll let you know anything I find out as soon as I can," I said.

"But..."

I hung up and picked up the other call before she could finish.

"Lucy! That you?"

"It is," I told Opal.

"I heard about what happened at your place last night. I'm so glad you're okay."

"Me too," I said.

"Anyway," she said. "This isn't an official call, but I just happened to glance at the report. Looks like the rifle shells were from Savage 300 cartridges."

"From whoever shot at me last night?"

"Yes," she said. "They were just outside your fence."

"So it was a rifle," I said. "Anything else?"

"Well," she said, "the fact that it was a rifle isn't the only interesting thing."

"What do you mean?"

"The casings are the same as the ones they found in that 'accidental shooting' all those years back."

"You mean Jimmy Karbach's death?"

"Exactly," she said.

"So you're thinking..."

"The only rifle that uses that kind of shell is a Savage Model 99, and there ain't too many of those around these days. Long and short of it is, I could be wrong," she said, "but I have an inklin' that whoever killed Jimmy Karbach thinks you've been askin' too many questions, and may be gunnin' for you now."

I HUNG UP A MINUTE LATER, feeling nauseated. Had I really been the target of a murderer? I looked at the hole in the wall, not far from where my head had been just as the shots had been fired.

Someone had killed Jo Nesbit. Was it the same person who had killed her father all those years ago?

And if they'd already killed two people, what would stop them from making it a hat trick?

I sat down at the table, my legs suddenly feeling weak. Chuck, sensing my upset, came over and leaned against my calf, looking up at me with solemn brown eyes. I petted his head, taking comfort in the soft fur, and tried to piece things together. I'd upset someone with my questions, that was for sure. But who?

Did Bitsy tell her brother and father I'd been by asking questions? And had one of them come to make sure I didn't ask any more?

I shivered to think of it.

As the sun began to drop, my nerves began jangling. I'd spent the day in the kitchen, making mozzarella balls and chèvre for the upcoming weekend's market, pouring another batch of mason-jar beeswax candles, and creating labels for a new blend of lavender-honey-scented soap I was experimenting with.

I was about to start cutting labels when I remembered the article I'd found in Jo's bedroom. Was there something else I'd missed in the Ulrich house? As I considered it, I thought I caught yet another whiff of lavender. Not enough to be sure, but enough to make me give the place a second look. Just in case.

I put the scissors down and headed out the back door, following the path to the gate and then walking down to the little house with the tin roof.

The door was firmly closed. I pulled out my key and let myself in, goosebumps rising on my skin at the thought of what I found last time I had entered this door.

I stepped into the shadowed interior, which looked just as it had the other day. Why was I here?

I walked through the living room, trying to imagine Alfie being in here with Jo, and wondering what had happened. She was still fully clothed when she passed, and the bed was still made. It didn't look like anything had happened between Alfie and Jo... at least not anything of an extramarital variety.

Wine. The bottle had been empty, and there were two glasses... but Alfie had said he hadn't taken the glass she offered, so she'd only poured one glass. There had been two glasses in the draining rack when I found her; someone else had been here. The glasses had been washed, but maybe there were prints on the wine bottle?

I pulled out my phone and called Opal, but there was no answer; I left a message and asked her to call me back as soon as she could.

22

My whole body relaxed when I saw Tobias's truck bumping down the driveway about a half hour later. Then I remembered that we were going to talk with the Greens, and I tensed up all over again.

I finished cutting out the label I had started, then stood up and walked over to meet Tobias at the door.

"Good day?" I asked as he stepped up on the porch, looking handsome as always in jeans and a dark blue T-shirt.

"It was, but successful. I managed to help deliver a litter of puppies and saved a cat who had been hit by a car, so I'm counting it a win."

"You're my hero," I said as he pulled me into a hug. "Are you hungry?" I asked as he released me. Chuck sat at our feet, almost falling over with wagging.

Tobias bent down and rubbed behind my poodle's floppy ears. "I am, but we should probably get the hard thing over with, don't you think?"

"I hear you, but I also think it's best to face things like this with something in your stomach."

"I can't argue with that logic," he said.

"I'll warm up some tomato pie and you can regale me with your heroic feats in animal care," I said as Chuck trotted behind us into the house.

A half hour later, we were both feeling refreshed. I slid the dishes into the dishwasher and was about to offer dessert when he said, "Okay. Time to do the hard thing."

"All right," I said. "What do we say?"

"We ask if they know anything about Jo Nesbit. If she got in touch with them, let them know her true identity."

"You think they're just going to tell us?" I asked.

"Of course not," he said. "But we know enough to be able to tell if they're lying."

"I forgot to tell you... Opal called off the record today, and told me the shells they found outside match the ones they found from that 'hunting accident' all those years ago."

His face turned solemn. "What kind of rifle?"

"A Savage Model 99," I said. "She said they weren't too common"

"They're not," he said. "In fact, they're really rare."

"That's what Opal said, too."

"Hmm," Tobias said. "I'd say odds are good whoever shot that rifle last night killed Jody Karbach."

"Well, I guess we can ask to see Bobby or Fred's gun collection while we're there," I said, half-jokingly.

"Whose house are we going to, anyway?" he asked.

"Jody told Alfie she had something on Bobby," I said.

"Then that's who we should go see first," he said.

"Oh, and I almost forgot... I realized today that Alfie told me Jody only poured wine for herself, but there were two glasses by the sink."

"So someone else was there after Alfie."

"That's what I'm thinking," I said.

"Might be nice to know what Bobby was up to the night Jody died."

"So we go in and ask to see his gun collection and then check his alibi?"

"Doesn't sound too promising, does it?" he asked.

I sighed. "Got any other ideas?"

"Sadly, no."

"You know, I actually do have one."

He looked at me, eyebrows raised. "What is it?"

"Mandy's always after me to write an article for the *Zephyr*. Since she's so involved with the case—they arrested her mother, after all—I'll say I'm writing the article, and wanted to know if he remembered Jody from when she was in high school and could add some local color for the article."

"Of course he knew Jody. Her dad had an affair with his mom."

I sighed again. "Got any other ideas?"

"Nope. So I guess we go with it."

"I guess so. Ready?"

"Not really," he said with a wry grin, "but we should probably get this over with."

THE GREENS LIVED on a big spread on the west side of town, heading toward LaGrange. Instead of having a gate, like a lot of locals, there were two limestone pillars flanking the entrance, with a cattle guard between them.

"At least they didn't get to turn us back at the gate," Tobias said, echoing my thoughts as we bumped over the metal bars and headed up the drive.

Although it was a long, winding drive through oaks and

mesquite trees, it seemed to be over way too soon, depositing us in front of what looked like a brick builder home. The two-story brick house, complete with a postage-stamp-sized green lawn, looked like it had been caught in a freak tornado and relocated from a Houston suburb to rural Buttercup. A red Ford F250 and a blue Hyundai Tucson were parked in the concrete driveway in front of the garage, and a portable soccer goal sat beside the house, a few balls scattered around the perimeter.

"Ready?" Tobias asked as we parked beside the Tucson.

"Here goes," I said, and together we got out of Tobias's truck.

I rang the doorbell and stood on the front porch sweating, and not just because it was 100 degrees in the shade.

Immediately, dogs began barking from somewhere within the house. A moment later, a teenaged girl opened the door, and two German Shepherds spilled out.

"Hey, guys!" Tobias said, squatting down to greet them. "Bo's looking really good," he said, stroking the bigger dog's back. "No sign of that cyst coming back, and the fur is growing in nicely."

"Thanks for taking care of it," the girl said.

"Happy to. I love that you guys take such good care of your dogs," he said approvingly as a man in jeans and a button-down Magellan shirt appeared at the door.

"Hi, Dr. Brandt," he said, smiling. I'd forgotten what an asset having a veterinarian boyfriend could be. "What brings you here?"

"Hey, Bobby," he said. "Sorry to just show up like this. Nothing to do with the dogs... I'm just keeping Lucy here company."

"Lucy Resnick," I said, holding a hand out. He shook it, but the smile faded.

"What can I do for you?" he asked. His daughter stood a few feet behind him, an alert expression on her round face. The family resemblance was obvious; they both had the same reddish hair, although hers had the vibrancy of youth, and their noses had a similar tilt.

"I hate to barge in on you like this," I said. "But Mandy Vargas has had some family trouble, and she asked me to take over writing an article on a woman who recently passed. Jo Nesbit, formerly Jody Karbach." His face hardened when I mentioned her name.

"Apparently she was in high school at the same time you were, and I was wondering if I could ask you a few questions... just your impression of her, for local color."

"You're a newspaper reporter?" his daughter asked, lighting up. "That's my dream job!"

"She worked for the Houston Chronicle for years," Tobias said, giving her his most winning smile. "I'm sure she'd be happy to take you to coffee and answer any questions."

"Oh, would you?" she asked.

"More than happy to!" I said. "We need more bright, young people like you in the field."

I could tell that every instinct in Bobby told him to shut the door in our faces, but now that his daughter was looking at me with shining eyes, he reluctantly opened it wider and invited us in.

"Thanks," I said.

"I'm Sarah, by the way," she told me as we followed them through the entry hall, which was cluttered with discarded soccer cleats and shin guards, into the big, open-plan living and dining area. Bob's Burgers was playing on the flat-screen TV, and a ten-year-old boy was ensconced on the sectional couch with a bag of goldfish. "And that's

Nathan," she said, with a dismissive nod toward her younger brother.

"Lucy Resnick," I said. "And this is Dr. Brandt."

"I know Dr. Brandt," she said, blushing a little bit. I resisted the urge to grin.

"Can I get you two something to drink?" Bobby asked.

"A glass of water would be great," I said. "It's hot out there."

"For me too, if it's not too much trouble," Tobias added.

As he filled two tumblers with ice and water, Sarah gave him a little hug. I could tell he was a family man. Could he really be responsible for suffocating Jody Karbach in the Ulrich house?

He put the glasses on the table and invited us to sit. Tobias and I took one side of the table, and he and Sarah sat down across from us. Although I was grateful to the young woman for easing our entry into the house, I was now wishing she and her brother would go outside and kick a few soccer balls so that we could talk to Bobby privately.

"All right," he said. "Sarah's got a soccer match in about an hour, so we don't have much time."

"It got postponed due to the heat, Daddy," she said. "We've got plenty of time."

He stifled a sigh. "Well, then. What can I do for you?"

I pulled a pen and pad out of the bag I'd brought with me and set them on the table. "I just wanted to ask you a few questions about Jody Karbach."

Again, his face grew stony.

"Local color stuff," I said, trying to put him more at ease. He had to know that I knew about his mother and Jody's dad. "What kind of person was she in high school?"

"I didn't really know her, to be honest," he said. "She wasn't here for long, and she was kind of a wallflower."

"So, no friends?"

He shook his head. "Like I said, I hardly knew her."

"No boyfriends? Anyone she was interested in?"

"Nope," he said.

"You told mom she had a thing for Alfie Kramer just the other day," Sarah corrected him. She looked at me, excited to be helping. "Like, she was totally obsessed with him. Remember? You were saying you thought that was why she came back to Buttercup in the first place."

"Sarah," he barked in a warning tone. She blinked, looking shocked.

"So you remember she had a crush on Alfie," I said. "Did he have any feelings for her?" I asked, feeling bad for even asking the question."

"Alfie was always about Molly," he answered. "Still is. I'm sorry I can't be more help."

"I appreciate it," I said. "But I have one more question. It's kind of a non sequitur… but from the look of your Facebook page, you're a big hunter. Do you happen to have a Savage Model 99 in your collection?"

"No," he said shortly.

"But…" Sarah said, and he cut her short with a look.

"You know, I think I've given you all I can," he said, pushing his chair back and standing up. "I've got some work to take care of. But thanks for stopping by."

"We still need to exchange our numbers…" Sarah protested.

"Another time," he said shortly.

Tobias and I looked at each other, then Sarah. Bobby's daughter stared at us, confused, then glanced at her father, who gave her a sharp head shake.

"Nice to meet you," she said in a quiet voice as Tobias and I followed her father to the door. I glanced back; the ten-year-old was still glued to the television, and Sarah followed a few feet behind us, looking worried.

"Thanks for having us," I said. "If you think of anything, please let me know." I scribbled my phone number on a piece of paper, tore it off the pad, and handed it to Bobby.

He looked at it as if I'd offered him a dirty tissue, then back at me. "Have a good day," he said, practically pushing us out the door and shutting it hard behind us.

As I took a step toward Tobias's truck, I heard Sarah's voice, muffled, from behind the door.

"What was that about? Why didn't you want them to know about grandpa's gun..."

"Enough," her father said tersely. We paused for a moment more, listening, but there was nothing else to be heard, so Tobias followed me back to the truck.

23

"Did you hear that?" I asked as soon as the truck door was shut tight behind me.

"The bit about grandpa's gun?" Tobias responded, putting the truck in reverse. "I did," he said. "That was a lot more productive than I thought it would be," he added, backing out of his parking spot.

"Thank goodness Sarah was there," I said as he then pointed the truck back down the winding driveway. "I think he would have shut the door in our faces otherwise."

"You think she'll get the number you gave him?"

"Maybe," I said. "And if not, she knows my name; I'm not too hard to find. If nothing else, she can ask you."

"He sure didn't want to talk about Jody, did he?" Tobias mused. "Or the gun."

"Do you think he's covering up for his father?" I asked.

"It kind of seems like he might be," Tobias said. "The problem is, how do we prove it?"

"I don't know," I said. "But I think we should tell Opal about it."

He sucked in his breath. "It's going to be hard to get a warrant."

"Probably," I said. "We should try anyway. What are the odds they'll let us get anywhere near Fred Green's property after our conversation today?"

"You're right," he said, and I picked up my phone to call the station.

"Buttercup sheriff's office, how can I help you?"

"Opal! It's Lucy."

"What's goin' on?"

"I found out who has a Savage Model 99," I told her. "Fred Green."

"How in the heck did you manage to figger that out?"

"We went and talked to Bobby. When I asked if they had a Savage Model 99, he escorted us out of the house, but once the door closed, I heard his daughter Sarah ask why he didn't want to talk about grandpa's gun."

"You are a sneaky one, aren't you?" she said. "Remind me not to kill anyone as long as you're in town. Even if Rooster does try my patience..."

I laughed.

"Anyway," she continued, "I don't know if we can convince the local judge to get a warrant for that, but let me call and see what I can do."

"We'd better move fast," I said.

"I'll talk to Rooster," she said with a deep sigh.

"Do you have to?"

"I do, I'm afraid. I'll call you back."

"Thanks," I told her, then hung up and turned to Tobias. "They're going to try to get a warrant."

"I don't have high hopes," he said.

"Opal and I don't either," I sighed. "I guess there's not much else we can do."

"It's late, but I think a quick nap would do us good," Tobias said, reaching out to put a hand on my knee. "I'm off till 10 at the clinic tomorrow; I had them cancel my early morning appointments. And neither of us got much sleep last night."

"No," I said. "I'm a little tired, that's true, and I've got the market on the square tomorrow, so I've got a lot to get ready tonight and early tomorrow morning. Picking veggies, labeling cheese, getting everything loaded onto the truck..."

"I can help you with that," he offered.

"Really? You're the best." I reached over and grabbed his hand. "I think you're right. Maybe it'll be easier to sleep when it's not dark outside."

"You're still on edge, aren't you?"

"I am," I said. "Aren't you?"

"I am," he confessed. "I'll be glad when this whole thing is over."

"I just hope we can get Rosita out of jail," I said.

"Me too. Maybe Opal will get a warrant, they'll find the gun, and he'll confess," he said, giving my leg a squeeze.

"Maybe," I said.

Unfortunately, that's not how it worked out.

Twenty minutes later, we were snuggled in bed with the curtains drawn, the fan on, and Chuck stationed on (admittedly sleepy) patrol duty at the foot of the bed. The cats, on the other hand, decided the curtain ties were fascinating, and kept skittering across the floor and meowing at each other as Tobias and I tried to catch some Zs.

He managed to drop off at once, one arm slung over me protectively. I was slower to doze off, so I grabbed Susan

Witting Albert's latest China Bayles mystery from the night table and attempted to lull myself to sleep with her words.

As charming as Pecan Springs was, however, my mind kept circling back to the rifle.

I'd visited Bobby under the impression that he had likely been the one to kill Jimmy Karbach... and shot up my home just the day before. Now, though, all of my assumptions were out the window.

Did Bobby know—or suspect—his father had killed Jimmy Karbach all those years ago, and had he been covering up for him for decades? And why hadn't I heard whoever shot into my kitchen coming or going? Chuck usually alerted me to anyone coming up the drive, and I saw and heard no sign of a vehicle.

I finally put down the book and grabbed my phone, pulling up Facebook and clicking on Bobby's page. His parents didn't have pages, but I hoped there might be something in his feed that would shake something loose for me.

I scrolled through the photos. Pictures of Sarah at her soccer games, a birthday photo at the kitchen of their home, with a big chocolate cake and fifteen yellow candles. Bitsy wasn't in the soccer photos, but she was in the birthday shot, a big smile on her face and a small, rainbow-wrapped gift in her hand as her niece blew out the candles, while her mother Alice looked on with her habitual slightly sour expression.

I kept scrolling. More soccer games, pictures of Bobby's new red truck... and then the familiar picture of Bitsy, Bobby and Fred in front of a dead buck. I wasn't a fan of hunting myself, even though I knew culling the herd helped with the deer overpopulation problem in Texas... but instead of scrolling past what to me was a distasteful photo, I found myself focusing on the firearm in Bitsy's hand.

"Bitsy takes her first buck of the season," read the caption below it. There were fifteen likes and six comments. Apparently not everyone shared my distaste for hunting photos.

I clicked on the photo and zoomed in on it, feeling gooseflesh prickle the back of my neck.

"Tobias," I said, nudging my sleeping boyfriend. "Look at this."

"What?" He asked, sitting up in a hurry, eyes darting around the room. "Is everything okay?"

"It is," I said. "But look at this." I showed him the zoomed-in photo of Bitsy with the deer.

"What about it?"

"What kind of rifle is that?" I asked.

He squinted and took the phone from me. "Oh," he said a moment later.

"It's the Savage Model 99, isn't it?"

"It is," he said. "Wow. That's practically a smoking gun."

"The question is, who has custody of it most of the time?"

I clicked on Bitsy's name again—she had been tagged in the post—and checked out her page a second time. There were several listings, of course, as well as the typical realtor glamor shots. I kept scrolling, hoping to find another picture of her and the Savage Model 99.

Six years back, I found it. A picture of Bitsy in pink camouflage and a diamond tennis bracelet, cradling the rifle.

"Look," I said, pointing to the captions.

"Starting this year's hunting season with my favorite rifle once again. Thanks, Daddy, for always being my best friend and believing in me. I'm still loving my "Sweet Sixteen" birthday gift all these years later!"

"Sweet Sixteen. Does that mean she had the rifle when Jody's dad died?"

"She was in the same year as Jody in high school, so that would put her at at least seventeen at the time."

"So the culprit turned out to be a dark horse."

"I still don't know how she managed to sneak up on us the other night," I said.

"She's a hunter," he said. "I'll bet she parked down by the road and walked up the drive."

"No wonder Chuck didn't react until the last minute," I said.

"I will never understand why people feel the need to put their whole lives on Facebook," Tobias said, shaking his head. "I'd screenshot this and send it to Opal. It should make the search warrant a slam dunk."

"Wouldn't it be nice if the police managed to solve this one without any further involvement from me?" I asked as I snapped a shot of the pic and texted it to Opal.

"Right?" he asked. "And now that you've solved the case... maybe we can find something else to occupy our afternoon?"

I laughed as he turned to kiss me. Chuck huffed from the bottom of the bed, and I had just put my arms around him when my little poodle began to growl.

"I'm sorry, buddy, but you're going to have to get used to PDAs," Tobias joked.

But Chuck wasn't growling at him. He sat up, staring at the curtained window, then leapt off the bed and raced toward the front door, toenails clicking on the hardwood.

"Someone's here," Tobias said.

24

"I didn't hear a car."

"Me neither," he said. "I'll go check it out; stay here."

"I'm coming with you," I said, already getting out of bed, but we hadn't reached the bedroom door before there was a loud crack.

"What was that?" I whispered. Chuck was going crazy, barking. I thought about what had happened the other night. Chuck, my faithful friend, was out there protecting us on his own, with no one to protect him.

"Chuck," I said, hurrying down the hallway and running toward the front door.

"Lucy!" Tobias hissed.

"I can't let him face whoever it is alone," I said over my shoulder.

"I'll get him," Tobias said, grabbing my arm. "Go call 911."

He didn't wait for me to answer. I paused for a moment, torn, but he was gone. I hurried back to the bedroom and grabbed my phone just as I heard the front door explode open, banging against the wall.

My heart was in my throat as I dialed 911. It seemed to take forever before a woman picked up.

"Fire, emergency or police?"

"There's an armed gunwoman at my house! I'm at Dewberry Farm in Buttercup."

"What's the address?" she asked.

I was about to reel it off when a woman's voice rang out at the door of the bedroom.

"Drop the phone!"

At the door stood Tobias, Chuck pressed to his chest, and Bitsy Hauser looming behind him. She was wearing camo—not pink this time, but the real deal—and holding the rifle I'd seen in her Facebook photos... the gift from her dear daddy.

I dropped the phone on the bed, but I didn't hang up.

"Bitsy Hauser," I said loudly, hoping the dispatcher could hear me. "What are you doing here?"

"Coming to take care of unfinished business," she said. "Go stand by your girlfriend," she ordered Tobias, poking him in the back with the rifle. He hurried over to me, thrust Chuck into my arms, then whirled around to put himself between the rifle and me.

"Such a gentleman," Bitsy said in a sarcastic tone. "Don't worry. I'll just shoot you first, and when you're down, I'll get her. I'm an excellent shot."

"I don't understand why you're here," I said.

"Oh, come off it. You were at my office yesterday, asking questions. I tried to take care of you last night, but I missed.

And then you went to my brother's house today, asking even more questions. You're starting to become a problem."

"In what way?" I asked, blinking in what I hoped was an innocent manner.

She rolled her eyes. "Oh, come on. You asked my brother about this rifle. I got a phone call right after you left."

"I think there must be some kind of misunderstanding," I said. "I was just writing an article for the *Zephyr* about what happened to Jo Nesbit and was looking for some local color from someone who went to school with her." Before I could come up with anything else to say, I heard "Ma'am? Are you there?" from the phone lying on the mussed bedcovers.

Bitsy's eyes narrowed as she zeroed in on the phone. "Hang it up and give it to me," she ordered.

I reached for the phone, hit the red button on the bottom of the screen and handed it to Bitsy, hoping the police were already en route.

"Who did you call?" she asked.

"I didn't get a chance to talk to anyone," I lied.

"Huh," she said, glancing down at the phone in her hand, then tossing it onto the bed. "Well, let's get this over with fast, just in case you're lying."

"You were the one who shot Jimmy all those years ago," I said, trying to stall for time. "In a 'hunting accident.' I thought it was your brother Bobby, or your father, until I remembered seeing that Facebook photo of you with the buck. Why did you do it?"

"Why did I do it? What else could I do?" she said, as if the answer were obvious. "That man ruined my family," she continued. "He was a lowlife from nowhere. When he seduced my poor mother, he made my family a laughing-stock. From that day on, all I heard at school were jokes about my mother. Lewd jokes. Disrespectful jokes. My family's reputation was ruined."

"You killed a man because of your family's reputation?"

"You don't understand," she hissed. "We went from being at the top of society to being the butt of jokes all the way to LaGrange; it took my mother a year before she could go to the Red & White Grocery without hanging her head in shame. And Daddy... I still don't think he's forgiven her."

"Still... why kill Jo?"

"Those Karbachs were the problem. If Jimmy Karbach and his white trash daughter had never come to Buttercup, my mother never would have been sweet-talked into making the biggest mistake of her life." She sniffled. "That man ruined my family. Ruined us. He deserved what he got."

From where I sat, her parents were still together, everyone in the family was relatively successful, and her mother had gotten over her shame to become Buttercup's code-enforcer-in-chief, with Bitsy following right in her footsteps, so things didn't look that dire to me. But I couldn't know how it had been for Bitsy twenty years ago... especially as a high-schooler in a small town.

"How did you find out Jo Nesbit was Jody Karbach?"

"She told me," she said. "After we inked the deal on the Rosita's building. And she said... she said she knew what had happened all those years ago, and that I'd better watch my step if I didn't want her to go to the police. I'd better work with her, make sure I brought her deals that were below-market if I wanted her to stay quiet." She gave a derogatory sniff. "Of course, she had it all wrong. Thought my brother was the one who shot her sorry excuse for a daddy. But Bobby's too soft. I always do the hard stuff. Always have."

"So you killed Jo, too?"

"I did, to protect the family, like always. She'd told Alfie she needed to talk to him, that she had some kind of proof my brother had killed her daddy. Alfie told Jody he was going to talk to her, but then he called Bobby and told him he left before she got to telling him what she knew. When my brother told me what happened, I knew what I had to do."

"You came over and killed her."

"I did," she said. "But first I told her I wanted to talk to her a bit. I wanted to find out what she knew, if anything, and if there was anything else I needed to clean up."

"Was there?"

"She knew about the rifle," she said. "I sat down with her, had her drink a few glasses while I talked about a building on the square that might be coming up soon, so she'd be easier to deal with. Then, after she was about three glasses in, I asked what exactly she thought she had on us. I knew she had something, but I didn't know what."

"And?"

"She said she knew my daddy owned a rifle just like the one that shot her daddy, so either he or Bobby must have been the one who killed him. She told me if I wanted her to keep quiet, I'd better keep feeding her deals."

"Did you have a glass of wine, too?"

"I poured one, but I didn't drink much. Just a sip or two. Then I washed up before I left."

"Clever. I keep wondering, though... How did you get up here? Both times? I didn't see or hear a car."

"I'm a hunter. I know about stalking prey," she said with a cruel smile. "The night I took care of Jo, I knew Alfie had been here, and chances were you'd seen his truck, so I parked down by the road and hoofed it up to where she was staying. And last night, I just played it the same way, so you wouldn't hear me coming."

"Smart," I said. I was still standing in my bedroom with Chuck in my arms, Tobias a few feet away from me. Would the police ever get here? If they didn't, how was I going to avoid being shot to death just like Jo's father? "I am curious, though. If you were drinking down in the living room, how did you get her up to the bedroom?" I asked. "You put a pillow over her face and smothered her, right?"

"Well, once we got through with her telling me all about how she thought my daddy shot her daddy, I told her I'd always been curious about the Ulrich house, but had never gotten a chance to see it. I asked her to give me a tour. She was more than happy to... but she was so sloshed she almost fell down the stairs on the way up. Drunkard, just like her daddy."

"So once you got upstairs, you pushed her onto the bed."

"I did," she confirmed. "And then I put a pillow on her face. She tried to scratch me, but I put my knees on her head and held her arms down with my hands." She made a face. "It took longer than I thought."

"And you were going to let Alfie take the fall for it?"

"I like Alfie," she said, "but family comes first, so if I had to, I would have. Honestly, though, I was glad when Rooster went after Rosita. One thing you can always count on in Buttercup, it's Rooster. He gets it wrong every time."

I couldn't disagree with her.

"I've been tryin' to decide what to do about Alfie, to be honest. I'm worried he might decide to tell the police something that will tie our family to what happened all those years ago. I told Bobby he needed to talk to Alfie, make sure he wasn't going to say anything."

I realized then that if we didn't get out of here alive, Alfie was almost certainly going to be next.

"So you did all this—shooting Jimmy Karbach, coming back years later and murdering Jo, then coming after me, all because you were worried about the family name,"

"Reputation is important," she said, drawing herself up. "Always has been, always will be. It's my responsibility to protect the Green family name." She adjusted the rifle, aiming it directly at Tobias. "And now, enough is enough. I have to decide how to handle you two. I've worked long and hard to protect the family, and I'm not about to let you take us down."

"You don't think they'll figure out it was you?" Tobias asked. "That's not an everyday kind of firearm you've got there," he said, indicating the rifle in her hands.

"You're right; that was an oversight on my part. But after this, I'm going to get rid of it; it's not registered anyway. And if they can't find the weapon, they can't link it to me, can they?" she added with a smirk. "Now come on." She jerked the barrel of the rifle toward the door. "You can leave the dog here. I would hate to hurt a defenseless animal," she said.

But you have no problem killing a human being who threatens your family's precious reputation, I thought, wondering how people managed to compartmentalize.

I bent to put Chuck down. At that moment, I felt a chill breeze pass through the room, along with a whiff of lavender. A banging sounded from the front of the house.

"What in the name of..." Bitsy turned toward the sound, distracted. At that moment, Tobias sprang at her. He shoved the barrel of the rifle upwards, away from us, and both of them tumbled through the open doorway to the floor of the hall.

Bitsy swore, trying to regain control of the gun. As the two wrestled on the runner in the hallway, I reached for the first thing I could find: the bedside lamp. Chuck barked wildly as I jerked the cord from the wall and closed the distance between Tobias and me. As I reached the hallway, Bitsy's head lifted in her attempt to yank the rifle back from Tobias. Her finger hit the trigger, and a bullet exploded into the wall a few inches from Tobias's head. At the same moment, I swung back with all my strength, and brought the lamp down on her chestnut hair.

She went limp immediately, sagging on top of Tobias. He pulled the rifle from her hand and handed it up to me, then rolled Bitsy off of him just as sirens sounded at the end of the driveway.

By the time the police had finished talking to us and took Bitsy, who had come around again, away in handcuffs, it was dark outside. After all the frenetic activity—the fear of being shot, the wondering if the police were coming, that terrifying moment when Tobias and Bitsy were wrestling for the gun—the quiet house seemed oddly anticlimactic.

I surveyed the new bullet hole in the bedroom hallway. "I guess I've got a good bit of repair work to do this fall," I said.

"Better the house than you," Tobias said. "Did you notice that weird breeze just before the end, by the way? And what was that banging noise?"

"This may sound kind of strange," I said, "but I think it was my grandmother coming to help."

"You talk to her?"

"I don't talk to her, no," I said, "but sometimes she's here. And she... well, she helps me out."

"That's pretty amazing," he said. "A little spooky, but amazing."

"It's not spooky at all," I told him. "She makes me feel loved."

"You are loved," he said, folding me into his arms. "I'm so glad nothing happened to you." He held me close, and I laid my head against his chest, listening to the beating of his heart and letting the tension drain out of me. After a long interval he drew a deep breath. "And I have to ask..." he began again, "are you okay with trying living together? Just to see how it goes?"

I lifted my head from his chest and looked up at him. "Here at the farm?" I asked.

"It seems to make more sense," he told me. "After today, I... I'll just sleep better knowing I'm here to protect you."

"I think I'd like that," I said.

"Good." He squeezed me even tighter, then kissed my forehead. "Now that that's settled, don't you have market days tomorrow?"

I groaned. "I nearly forgot. I haven't even picked produce."

"Let's get everything else ready and I can help you with that first thing in the morning, when it's light enough to see."

"Are you sure?" I asked.

"Absolutely," he said. "You don't have to do everything yourself, you know. I'm here to help."

His words made my heart open, and warmth coursed through me. I did always try to do everything by myself, as if my independence could protect me somehow. I'd had my heart hurt before, and I think I was afraid to open it completely again.

But now, with Tobias here, I decided I was ready to really take the risk and see what happened. After all, what's life without someone to share it with?

"Okay," I said with a grin. "You're on. But which one of us is going to pick the okra?"

25

Despite all the craziness of the previous day, Tobias helped me load up the truck.

"Thanks so much for helping me," I said as he lugged the cooler full of cheese to the back of the truck and put up the tailgate for me. "And for being there yesterday."

"You are my priority," he said. "I wouldn't have wanted to be anywhere else."

"Even with Bitsy waving around her antique rifle?"

"Especially with Bitsy waving around her antique rifle," he said with a grin, and pulled me into a hug. "Think you can make it through the market without getting involved in another murder case?"

"I'll do my best," I said, smiling. "Let's hope I manage to sell all this cheese, though. I'm still sad I don't have eggs. Or chickens." My heart wrenched as I thought of my missing flock. Were they on someone's dinner table by now? I hated to think of it.

He gave me a kiss and walked me to the driver's seat of the truck. "I finish up at noon and I'll stop by the market to help you load up again."

"You're amazing," I told him, and I was still smiling when I got to the end of the driveway and headed toward town.

My stall today was next to Peter's, which made me happy. Quinn had started selling some of her famous maple twists on consignment with him. Once I finished laying out my soaps and beeswax candles, I arranged the glossy eggplants, cherry tomatoes, okra, and cucumbers I had managed to wrest from my water-starved veggie patch. I finished by setting out little cups of chèvre and mozzarella bites for customers to sample and then went next door to Green Haven farm to indulge in some of Quinn's maple twists before they sold out.

"Hey Peter!" I said as I snagged a bag for Tobias and me.

"Hi there, Lucy! I saw Mandy a few minutes ago... congrats on cracking another case! She told me you have a job whenever you want it."

"Well, if farming continues to go like it has this year, I may have to take her up on it." I reached for my wallet to pay for the maple twists, but Peter told me they were on the house. "Consider it a reward for catching a murderer," he said with a grin.

"Aw, thanks!" I said. "If only I had the same luck finding the chickennappers!"

"I know," he said, his smile fading. "I'm still heartbroken over it. I hate thinking of Love Chick and Girly Girl ending up on someone's dinner table."

"I feel the same way about Niblet and Hester," I said. As I spoke, a flash of hot pink at Bubba's Barbecue stall caught my eye. "Is that Flora?" I asked, watching the swirl of pink moving toward us.

"It is," he said. "I haven't seen her dressed like that in a while."

"Flora!" I called as she came close enough to hear me. "You look amazing!"

"Thanks," she said, the roses back in her cheeks as she smiled. "You're not going to believe what happened."

"What?"

"Gus sent me ten dozen roses and then showed up with a diamond necklace," she said, beaming. "Then he told me he didn't care where he lived as long as it was with me."

"That's so romantic!"

"Isn't it? I felt like a princess. He also told me I could donate every last nickel of my mama's money to a pot-bellied pig rescue and he'd still want to spend the rest of his life with me."

"And what did you say?" I asked, although I already knew an answer.

"I told him I was sorry for being mean as a mama's wasp, but after what happened with my last beau..." She held up her left hand, and a diamond once again sparkled on her third finger.

"So the wedding's back on?"

"It is," she said. "Gus is the best thing that ever happened to me. I think I had to spend some time without him to realize just how much he means to me." As I admired her ring—and the diamond pendant glittering above her bodice—the man himself came up behind Flora, looking smart in snakeskin boots and a gold belt buckle the size of a dinner plate.

"Howdy, Lucy," he said, tipping his straw hat.

"I hear there's some news to celebrate," I said, grinning.

"She took me back," he said, his own face splitting into a smile. "Thank the lord. I don't know what I'd do without her."

"I'm so happy for you both," I said, as he put his arms around her and pulled her into a hug.

"I hear you went to plead my case," he said.

"I did," I said. "Nothing as persuasive as several dozen roses and a diamond necklace, I'm afraid, but Flora did help me."

"How?" she asked.

"I found out about Jo Nesbit's real estate activities. It was another piece of the puzzle."

"I heard you and Dr. Brandt had a showdown with that crazy Bitsy at Dewberry Farm," Gus said. "Shot out half the windows."

"She did," I said.

"I'm glad she missed you," Gus said. "We like having you around... and Dr. Brandt, too."

"You two gonna get hitched anytime soon?" Flora asked with a mischievous grin.

I laughed. "One wedding at a time," I said. "Otherwise, Mary at the Enchanted Florist won't be able to keep up."

"Funny you should mention her. I went to talk about wedding flowers this morning, and she told me she needed a silent partner. Gus and I thought it would be a good use of Mama's money to support local business, so we're talkin' about workin' out a loan on favorable terms so she can keep the doors open."

"Oh, that's wonderful news," I said.

"We've still got a few things to iron out," she said, "but I think we can make it work."

"That's terrific," I told her. "Any idea what's going to happen to Rosita's?"

"I heard just last night that the sale hadn't closed yet."

"I heard that, too."

"Anyhow, turns out Jody Karbach comin' in and settin'

new terms was puttin' the cart before the horse. So Rosita's lookin' to sell some family land they've got down in Brazoria County and use that to buy the building."

"Then they don't have the rent issue anymore," I said. "That's great news."

"Well, it's still early days, but we'll see," she said. "Anyhow, I hope we can have lunch one day soon at the Blue Onion. I've got some new ideas for the wedding I want to run by you."

"Anytime," I said. "I'm just so glad to see you two back together again."

"So am I," Gus said. "I waited more than fifty years to meet this young lady. It'd be an awful shame to lose her."

Flora beamed. I gave each of them a hug and watched them walk, hand in hand, through the rest of the market.

THE MARKET WAS in full swing, and I was down to two pints of cherry tomatoes and had sold more than half my cheese when Quinn swung by.

"How's it going?" she asked.

"Sales are good," I said. "My stomach's rumbling for a chopped beef sandwich from Bubba's, though."

"Want me to keep an eye on the booth for a few minutes?"

"That would be great," I said. "I won't be long."

"Take your time," she said.

My first stop was Bubba's. Once I had my sandwich in hand (chopped brisket with tangy sauce and lots of sweet onion slices on top... mmm), I headed for the little seating area under a pop-up awning on the green area in front of the square. I was sinking my teeth into my sandwich when my eyes drifted to a stall I'd never seen before.

"Pastured Eggs $10/dozen" read the hand-lettered sign. A young man in a red T-shirt was standing at a gingham-clad table with a long line of shoppers; despite the outrageous price he was asking for the eggs, he was very much in demand, and from what I'd seen, he was the only egg vendor at the market.

I watched him pull another dozen eggs from a cooler as I finished my sandwich and wiped a bit of sauce off my chin with a napkin.

I knew all the farmers at the market—there weren't very many of us—but this one was brand new. I tossed my sandwich wrapper into a trash can and walked toward the booth, giving it a wide berth. As I watched, he pulled another carton of eggs from a cooler, then excused himself for a moment and ducked out the back of the booth. I picked up the pace, watching to see where he went. Behind him was a black truck. There was no cage in the back now, but I could see the license plate. The first three digits were the same as the ones I'd spotted on the van at Green Haven farm.

I pulled out my phone and snapped a few surreptitious shots of both the van and the young man in the red shirt, then texted them to Opal.

A moment later, she texted back. "Sending Deputy Shames right now."

I hung back, even though I was dying to go ask the man if he was the one who had stolen all of my chickens... and if they were still alive somewhere.

After what seemed like forever, the familiar form of Deputy Shames appeared, dressed in her full uniform. The young man's eyes widened in alarm when she hailed him.

He blinked a few times in confusion, then excused himself to go to his truck. As Deputy Shames watched, he went to the passenger side, I was guessing to pull out proof of registration. But instead of coming back, he hurled himself into the driver's seat, revved the engine, and tore out of his parking place, turning left at the gates to head toward Highway 71.

Deputy Shames pulled out her radio and barked what looked like a few urgent words into it as she sprinted toward a cruiser parked on the far end of the square. Another officer I didn't recognize turned up at the now-deserted booth a moment later, directing the would-be patrons to move on.

I hurried over to where Peter was taking money for a bag of organic black-eyed peas. "The chickennapper was here!" I announced.

"Here?" He looked up and around. "Where?"

"They were selling eggs at a booth across the square," I said. "I recognized the truck and texted a picture of it to Opal; she put Deputy Shames on it. I saw her go talk to the guy. He hopped in his truck and took off in a hurry; she's in pursuit now."

Peter's face lit up. "Just eggs? No chickens for sale?"

"Not that I saw," I said.

"So we might see Girly Girl and Love Chick again after all?"

"And Niblet and Hester," I said. "Fingers crossed."

"I knew it wasn't time to get new chicks!" Quinn said, tucking a stray curl back into her bandanna as she finished ringing up a cheese purchase to a young family. "Can you get in touch with Opal now that you have the license plate and find out where the truck is registered?" she asked.

I texted Opal the question. A moment later, she texted that she'd sent the address to Deputy Shames and that if the deputy didn't manage to catch up with the driver, she'd go to the address linked with the truck. "Apparently the truck's registered to an address in LaGrange," I told Peter and Quinn as I read her last missive.

"I just hope they find them all," Peter said. "I miss them."

"Me too," I said as another group of shoppers drifted by.

"Would you like to try some cheese?" Quinn offered them.

She sold them a few tubs of chèvre as I busied myself behind the table, refilling the candle and soap supplies.

"Did Peter tell you about Gus and Flora?" I asked Quinn when she'd finished.

"He did! And she's going to help out Mary at the Enchanted Florist, too, he told me."

"It's great, isn't it?"

"I just hope Rosita figures out some way to hold onto the building," Quinn said.

As she spoke, my phone lit up. It was Mandy Vargas.

"Hey, Mandy!" I said, picking up.

"I know you're in the middle of the market right now," she said, "but I wanted to invite you and Tobias to my mom and dad's for a celebratory dinner tonight."

"I'll check with Tobias, but that sounds terrific."

"I'm so glad you figured out what happened and saved my mom," she said. "Do you think I could talk you into writing an article on it for the *Zephyr*?"

"Maybe," I said.

"I'd love to have you on staff. It might help to have a second source of income, after all. And you have a great nose for investigative reporting."

"Thanks," I said, trying to decide how I felt about dipping into the profession I'd left behind in Houston a few years back. "How about I think about it and get back to you?" I asked.

"The door is always open," she said. "And I hope to see you tonight. My mom's making carnitas to celebrate, and I'm bringing homemade *agua de sandía*."

I loved *agua de sandía*, or watermelon water; the mix of pureed watermelon, water, sugar and a touch of lime was the perfect drink for a hot evening in Texas.

I glanced at my watch; Tobias would be back to the market in an hour. "Can I call you at around 1:30 and let you know?"

"Of course," she said. "And Lucy, thank you again. Without you..."

"I am so glad I could help," I said.

TOBIAS ARRIVED fifteen minutes after the market ended, just in time to help me load the truck. I'd sold all my veggies, half the soap, and was down to two tubs of chèvre and one of mozzarella; it had been a good day.

"Mandy invited us over to her parents' house for dinner," I told him. "Carnitas and *agua de sandía*."

"What can we bring?" he asked.

"I'll ask when I tell her we'll be there," I said. "And there's more news, too!" I told him about running into Gus and Flora and the egg seller with the familiar pick-up truck. "I still haven't heard back from Opal or Deputy Shames, but I'm hoping this means we'll be able to find our flocks."

"Here's hoping," he said, pulling me into a hug, then reaching for the nearest cooler. "Homeward bound?"

"Absolutely," I said. "And I got a dozen of Quinn's maple twists before they sold out!"

We said our goodbyes to Peter and Quinn, promising to have them over soon, and headed back to Dewberry Farm. It had been a good day. I was just hoping we'd have some more good news about Niblet and the rest of the chickens to top it off.

26

I had just gotten home and finished unloading the truck when the phone rang. It was Molly.

I took a deep breath and answered. "Hey," I said in a tentative voice. "You okay?"

"I talked with Alfie," she said, her voice gravelly. "We're... we're good. Or working on things."

"Oh, Molly," I breathed, not realizing how much tension I'd been holding. "I'm so sorry I didn't say anything earlier. I just... I didn't know what to do."

"I understand," she said. "But I'm still shaken. By both of you. I... I trust the two of you more than anyone else. I don't like that you hid things from me."

"I get it," I said. "I'm so sorry. I should have told you."

"You should have," she agreed. "And so should Alfie." She took a deep breath. "I know he was protecting his friend, but I thought we shared everything. Now... well, we're going to have to rebuild."

"I'm so sorry you're hurt," I said, "and I'm sorry I was part of it. "But I'm glad you two are talking. I would hate for this to pull you apart; you've built such an amazing life together, and your relationship has always been something of an inspiration, if I'm honest."

"Really?" she said.

"Really," I told her. "I see the way Alfie looks at you and I hope I find someone who looks at me that way."

"Um… Lucy," she said. "You have."

"Tobias?" I queried, feeling my heart flutter.

"Absolutely," she said. It was surprisingly good to hear; I felt my face flush and my heart pick up the pace. "Anyway," she said, "I've got to go, but I just wanted to say… I forgive you."

"You do?" I said, my limbs loose with release.

"I do," she said. "But next time? Tell me."

"I will," I promised, and hung up the phone feeling grateful for the grace of good friends… and hoping I never had to face a situation that sticky again.

And more than anything, I was glad Molly and Alfie were committed to working things out. Their relationship was too precious for a mishap like this one to tear it apart. I was beyond relieved they were willing to mend it.

#

By the time we got in my truck to head to the Vargas's house that night, we'd found out that all of the missing chickens had been located, and were safe and sound.

"Apparently with egg prices goin' through the roof, some bright bulb decided to corner the market on production," Opal said. "So they just went around stealin' everybody's flock and storin' them in an old barn outside of LaGrange."

"How are we going to figure out who's who?" I asked.

"He kept 'em separate," Opal said, "so they wouldn't peck each other to death."

"Smart," I said. "When can I come get them?"

"Well, they're kind of evidence right now," she said, "but

I think by tomorrow you can come retrieve them all. Of course, chickens ain't worth much, so it'll probably just be a misdemeanor, but at least we got your girls back."

"That's all I care about, honestly," I said.

"So all's well that ends well," Opal said. "And you managed to not get your head shot off."

"I did," I said. "No hunting accidents. Any word on what's going on with Bitsy?"

"She's denyin' everything, of course, but the coroner found a little bit of skin under Jo's fingernails, so we're guessing she managed to get a good scratch in before she expired. We're runnin' the DNA and there's a good chance it'll come up with a match."

"What about the 'hunting accident' involving Jody's father?"

"Well, we've got your statement," she said, "and the gun she was holding matched. No promises, of course, Rooster bein' Rooster, but I'm hopin' she'll be charged for that murder, too."

"Poor Jody," I said. "What a tragic life."

"True, but if she hadn't come back and tried to make life miserable for everyone she knew in high school, she might have been able to move on," Opal said.

"That's true," I agreed. "But no one should have to lose a father like that."

"You're not wrong," Opal said. "We can't go back and help Jody, and I'm sad the sheriff didn't do enough to see justice done way back then, but at least we can make sure her killer winds up where she belongs. And that poor Rosita doesn't have to spend the rest of her life payin' for a crime she didn't commit."

"I guess you're right," I said. "And Jody wasn't the nicest person either, if you get right down to it."

"No, she wasn't. She didn't deserve what happened to her, but she wasn't an angel herself." Opal sighed. "I guess nothin's perfect in this world. We just all have to do the best we can. And Lucy?"

"Yeah?"

"You done good."

DESPITE MY SADNESS OVER JODY, my heart warmed at the welcome we received at the Vargases' house that night. We'd brought a twelve pack of Shiner Bock, and I'd whipped up a quick batch of chocolate chip cookies to add to the table.

"Oh, Lucy," Mandy said, greeting me at the door. "I can't thank you enough. If it hadn't been for you, this wouldn't be possible." She turned to my handsome boyfriend, who was standing right behind me holding the Shiner. "And you, too, Tobias... I hear you wrestled Bitsy to the ground!"

"It was Lucy who knocked her out with a lamp," he said.

"It was a team effort," I said.

"Come in, come in!" Mandy said, opening the door wide. I could smell the smoky, spicy scent of carnitas, and my mouth began watering. "Can I get you a drink?"

"Got any of that *agua sandía*?" I asked.

"All you can drink," she said. "Follow me to the kitchen. My mom wants to give you a hug!"

We spent the next few hours drinking sweet, cool *agua sandía* (me) and Shiner Bock (Tobias), devouring carnitas wrapped in fresh tortillas and topped with onion, cilantro, and Rosita's special green salsa, and getting hugs from everyone in the Vargas family.

"I hear you may have a way of buying the restaurant building?" I asked Rosita as she offered me a fourth helping of carnitas. Chiquis, her low-slung dachshund, was hovering at her feet; as I watched, she slipped him a chunk of pork, which he dispatched quickly.

"We have some family land," she said. "It has been in the family for generations, but we are thinking it may be time to sell it. We're talking to agents right now... I am hoping we can make a deal so we never have to have a landlord again!"

"That would be amazing," I said.

"All these people coming in and changing Buttercup, trying to make it like... like the Houston Galleria. We need to keep some of the town for ourselves, don't you think?"

"Absolutely," Tobias said. "I've had three corporate vet clinics offer to buy me out in the past year, but I prefer to stay local."

"I'm glad," Rosita said. "And by the way, I need to bring Chiquis in for a check-up this week. Ernesto thinks he's getting a little *gordo*, but I don't think so, do you?"

We looked down at the little brown dachshund, who was so round his belly brushed the floor, and I burst out laughing.

"I'll bet you fifty bucks Tobias has Chiquis on the carrot and cucumber diet by Tuesday, just like Chuck," I said.

"It's for their own good..." Tobias started.

"Oh, Tobias," Rosita said, shaking her head and slipping another piece of pork to Chiquis, who wolfed it down and looked up for more. "Life is too short to not eat the tacos."

"I'll be by to pick up my fifty bucks on Wednesday," I grinned, feeling grateful beyond measure that Rosita—and Rosita's—were here in Buttercup to stay.

THE END

MURDER ON THE ROCKS
CHAPTER ONE

Hungry for more adventures? Escape to the Gray Whale Inn on quaint Cranberry Island, Maine!

Here's a sneak preview of the Agatha-nominated Murder on the Rocks, first in Karen's beloved ten-book (and counting) Gray Whale Inn cozy mystery series. **Now on Kindle Unlimited!**

Chapter One

The alarm rang at 6 a.m., jolting me out from under my down comforter and into a pair of slippers. As much as I enjoyed innkeeping, I would never get used to climbing out of bed while everyone else was still sleeping. Ten minutes later I was in the kitchen, inhaling the aroma of dark-roasted coffee as I tapped it into the coffeemaker and gazing out the window at the gray-blue morning. Fog, it looked like—the swirling mist had swallowed even the Cranberry Rock lighthouse, just a quarter of a mile away. I grabbed the sugar and flour canisters from the pantry and dug a bag of blueberries out of the freezer for Wicked Blueberry Coffee Cake. The recipe was one of my favorites: not only did my guests rave over the butter-and-brown-sugar-drenched cake, but its simplicity was a drowsy cook's dream.

The coffeepot had barely finished gurgling when I sprinkled the pan of dimpled batter with brown-sugar topping and eased it into the oven. My eyes focused on the clock above the sink: 6:30. Just enough time for a relaxed thirty minutes on the kitchen porch.

Equipped with a mug of steaming French-roast coffee, I grabbed my blue windbreaker from its hook next to the door and headed out into the gray Maine morning. As hard as it was to drag myself out of a soft, warm bed while it was still dark outside, I loved mornings on Cranberry Island.

I settled myself into a white-painted wooden rocker and took a sip of strong, sweet coffee. The sound of the waves crashing against the rocks was muted, but mesmerizing. I inhaled the tangy air as I rocked, watching the fog twirl around the rocks and feeling the kiss of a breeze on my cheeks. A tern wheeled overhead as the thrum of a lobster boat rumbled across the water, pulsing and fading as it moved from trap to trap.

"Natalie!" A voice from behind me shattered my reverie. I jumped at the sound of my name, spilling coffee on my legs. "I was looking for you." Bernard Katz's bulbous nose protruded from the kitchen door. I stood up and swiped at my coffee-stained jeans. I had made it very clear that the kitchen was off-limits to guests—not only was there a sign on the door, but it was listed in the house rules guests received when they checked in.

"Can I help you with something?" I couldn't keep the anger from seeping into my voice.

"We're going to need breakfast at seven. And my son and

his wife will be joining us. She doesn't eat any fat, so you'll have to have something light for her."

"But breakfast doesn't start until 8:30."

"Yes, well, I'm sure you'll throw something together." He glanced at his watch, a Rolex the size of a life preserver. "Oops! You'd better get cracking. They'll be here in twenty minutes."

I opened my mouth to protest, but he disappeared back into my kitchen with a bang. My first impulse was to storm through the door and tell Katz he could fish for his breakfast, but my business survival instinct kicked in. Breakfast at seven? Fine. That would be an extra $50 on his bill for the extra guests—and for the inconvenience. Scrambled egg whites should do the trick for Mrs. Katz Jr. First, however, a change of clothes was in order. I swallowed what was left of my coffee and took a deep, lingering breath of the salty air before heading inside to find a fresh pair of jeans.

My stomach clenched again as I climbed the stairs to my bedroom. Bernard Katz, owner of resorts for the rich and famous, had earmarked the beautiful, and currently vacant, fifty-acre parcel of land right next to the Gray Whale Inn for his next big resort—despite the fact that the Shoreline Conservation Association had recently reached an agreement with the Cranberry Island Board of Selectmen to buy the property and protect the endangered terns that nested there. The birds had lost most of their nesting grounds to people over the past hundred years, and the small strip of beach protected by towering cliffs was home to one of the largest tern populations still in existence.

Katz, however, was keen to make sleepy little Cranberry Island the next bijou in his crown of elite resorts, and was throwing bundles of money at the board to encourage them to sell it to him instead. If Katz managed to buy the land, I was afraid the sprawling resort would mean the end not only for the terns, but for the Gray Whale Inn.

As I reached the door to my bedroom, I wondered yet again why Katz and his assistant were staying at my inn. Bernard Katz's son Stanley and his daughter-in-law Estelle owned a huge "summer cottage" called Cliffside that was just on the other side of the preserve. I had been tempted to decline Katz's reservation, but the state of my financial affairs made it impossible to refuse any request for a week in two of my most expensive rooms.

I reminded myself that while Katz and his assistant Ogden Wilson were odious, my other guests—the Bittles, a retired couple up from Alabama for an artists' retreat—were lovely, and deserved a wonderful vacation. And at least Katz had paid up front. As of last Friday, my checking account had dropped to under $300, and the next mortgage payment was due in two weeks. Although Katz's arrival on the island might mean the eventual end of the Gray Whale Inn, right now I needed the cash.

Goosebumps crept up my legs under the wet denim as I searched for something to wear. Despite the fact that it was June, and one of the warmer months of the year, my body hadn't adjusted to Maine's lower temperatures. I had spent the last fifteen years under Austin's searing sun, working for the Texas Department of Parks and Wildlife and dreaming of someday moving to the coast to start a bed-and-breakfast.

I had discovered the Gray Whale Inn while staying with a friend in a house she rented every summer on Mount Desert Island. I had come to Maine to heal a broken heart, and had no idea I'd fall in love all over again—this time with a 150-year-old former sea captain's house on a small island accessible only by boat.

The inn was magical; light airy rooms with views of the

sea, acres of beach roses, and sweet peas climbing across the balconies. I jotted down the real estate agent's number and called on a whim, never guessing that my long-term fantasy might be within my grasp. When the agent informed me that the inn was for sale at a bargain price, I raced to put together enough money for a down payment.

I had had the good fortune to buy a large old house when Austin was a sleepy town in a slump. After a room-by-room renovation, it sold for three times the original price, and between the proceeds of the house and my entire retirement savings, there was just enough money to take out a mortgage on the inn. A mortgage, I reflected as I strained to button my last pair of clean jeans, whose monthly payments were equivalent to the annual Gross National Product of Sweden.

I tossed my coffee-stained jeans into the overflowing laundry basket and paused for a last-minute inspection in the cloudy mirror above the dresser. Gray eyes looked back at me from a face only slightly plump from two months of butter-and sugar-laden breakfasts and cookies. I took a few swipes at my bobbed brown hair with a brush and checked for white hairs—no new ones today, although with the Katzes around my hair might be solid white by the end of the summer. If I hadn't already torn all of my hair out, that is.

When I pushed through the swinging door to the dining room at 7:00, Bernard Katz sat alone, gazing out the broad sweep of windows toward the section of coastline he had earmarked for his golf course. He looked like a banker in a blue pinstriped three-piece suit whose buttons strained to cover his round stomach. Katz turned at the sound of my footsteps, exposing a line of crooked teeth as he smiled. He was a self-made man, someone had told me. Apparently there'd been no money in the family budget for orthodontic work. Still, if I had enough money to buy islands, I'd have found a couple of thousand dollars to spare for straight teeth.

"Coffee. Perfect." He plucked the heavy blue mug from the place setting in front of him and held it out. "I'll take cream and sugar." I filled his cup, congratulating myself for not spilling it on his pants, then plunked the cream pitcher and sugar bowl on the table.

"You know, you stand to earn quite a bit of business from our little project." Katz took a sip of coffee. "Not bad," he said, sounding surprised. "Anyway, there's always a bit of overflow in the busy season. We might be able to arrange something so that your guests could use our facilities. For a fee, of course."

Of course. He leaned back and put his expensively loafered feet on one of my chairs. Apparently he was willing to cough up some change for footwear. "I know starting a business is tough, and it looks like your occupancy is on the low side." He nodded at the room full of empty tables.

"Well, it is an hour and a half before breakfast." He didn't have to know that only two other rooms were booked —and one of those was for Barbara Eggleby, the Shoreline Conservation Association representative who was coming to the island for the sole purpose of preventing his development from happening.

"Still," he went on, "this is the high season." His eyes swept over the empty tables. "Or should be. Most of the inns in this area are booked to capacity." My first impulse was to respond that most of the inns in the area had been open for more than two months, and that he was welcome to go to the mainland and stay at one of them, but I held my tongue.

He removed his feet from my chair and leaned toward

me. "Our resort will make Cranberry Island *the* hot spot for the rich and famous in Maine. Kennebunkport won't know what hit it. Your place will be perfect for the people who want glitz but can't afford the price tag of the resort."

Glitz? The whole point of Cranberry Island was its ruggedness and natural beauty. So my inn would be a catchall for poor people who couldn't quite swing the gigantic tab at Katz's mega resort. Lovely.

I smiled. "Actually, I think the island works better as a place to get away from all the 'glitz'. And I don't think a golf course would do much to enhance the island's appeal." I paused for a moment. "Or the nesting success of the black-chinned terns."

"Oh, yes, the birds." He tsked and shook his head. The sun gleamed on his bald pate, highlighting the liver spots that had begun to appear like oversized freckles. "I almost forgot, you're heading up that greenie committee. I would have thought you were smarter than that, being a business-woman." He waved a hand. "Well, I'm sure we could work something out, you know, move the nests somewhere else or something."

"Good morning, Bernie." The sharp report of stiletto heels rescued me from having to respond. *Bernie?*

"Estelle!" Katz virtually leaped from his chair. "Please, sit down." Katz's daughter-in-law approached the table in a blaze of fuchsia and decorated Katz's cheeks with two air kisses before favoring him with a brilliant smile of straight, pearl-white teeth. Clearly orthodontic work had been a priority for her. Her frosted blonde hair was coiffed in a Marilyn Monroe pouf, and the neckline of her hot pink suit plunged low enough to expose a touch of black lace bra. An interesting choice for a foggy island morning on the coast of Maine. Maybe this was what Katz meant by glitz.

She turned her ice-blue eyes to me and arranged her frosted pink lips in a hard line. "Coffee. Black." She returned her gaze to Katz, composing her face into a simpering smile as he pulled out a chair for her.

"Estelle, I'm so glad you could come. Where's Stanley?" Stanley Katz was Bernard Katz's son, and Estelle's husband. I'd seen him around the island; he had inherited his father's girth and balding pate, but not his business sense or charisma. Stanley and Estelle had seemed like a mismatched couple to me until I found out the Katzes were rolling in the green stuff. As much as I didn't like the Katzes, I felt sorry for Stanley. Between his overbearing father and his glamorous wife, he faded into the background.

"Stanley?" Estelle looked like she was searching her brain to place the name. "Oh, he's out parking the car. I didn't want to have to walk over all of those horrid rocks." She fixed me with a stare. "You really should build a proper walkway. I could have broken a heel."

Katz chuckled. "When the Cranberry Island Premier Resort is built, you won't have to worry about any rocks, my dear." Or birds, or plants, or anything else that was "inconvenient." Their voices floated over my shoulder as I headed back to the kitchen. "You look stunning as usual, Estelle."

"Keep saying things like that and I'll be wishing I'd married *you*!" I rolled my eyes as the kitchen door swung shut behind me. The aroma of coffee cake enveloped me as I ran down my mental checklist. Fruit salad, whole wheat toast, and skinny scrambled eggs for Estelle; scrambled whole eggs and blueberry coffee cake would work for Katz, who from the bulge over his pin-striped pants didn't seem too interested in Weight Watchers-style breakfasts. I tugged at the snug waistband of my jeans and grimaced. At least Katz and I had one thing in common. I grabbed a crystal bowl from the cabinet and two melons from the countertop.

As the French chef's knife sliced through the orange flesh of a cantaloupe, my eyes drifted to the window. I hoped the blanket of fog would lift soon. The Cranberry Island Board of Selectmen was meeting tonight to decide what to do with the land next door, and Barbara Eggleby, the Shoreline Conservation Association representative, was due in today. I was afraid the bad weather might delay her flight. *Save Our Terns*, the three-person island group I had formed to save the terns' nesting ground from development, was counting on Barbara for the financial backing to combat Katz's bid for development. As I slid melon chunks into the bowl and retrieved a box of berries from the refrigerator, my eyes returned to the window. The fog did look like it was letting up a bit. I could make out a lobster boat chugging across the leaden water. The berries tumbled into a silver colander like dark blue and red gems, and as the water from the faucet gushed over them, the small boat paused to haul a trap. A moment later, the engine growled as the boat turned and steamed toward the mainland, threading its way through the myriad of brightly colored buoys that studded the cold saltwater.

Since moving to the island, I had learned that each lobsterman had a signature buoy color that enabled him to recognize his own traps, as well as the traps of others. I had been surprised to discover that what I thought of as open ocean was actually carved up into unofficial but zealously guarded fishing territories.

My eyes followed the receding boat as I gave the berries a final swirl and turned off the faucet. Lately, some of the lobstermen from the mainland had been encroaching on island territory, and the local lobster co-op was in an uproar.

I strained my eyes to see if any of the offending red and green buoys were present. The veil of fog thinned for a moment, and sure enough, bobbing next to a jaunty pink and white one was a trio of what looked like nautical Christmas ornaments.

The boat had vanished from sight by the time the fruit salad was finished. I eyed my creation—the blueberries and raspberries interspersed with the bright green of kiwi made a perfect complement to the cantaloupe—and opened the fridge to retrieve a dozen eggs and some fat-free milk. When I turned around, I slammed into Ogden Wilson, Katz's skinny assistant. My fingers tightened on the milk before it could slip from my grasp, but the impact jolted the eggs out of my hand. I stifled a curse as the carton hit the floor. Was I going to have to install a lock on the kitchen door?

Ogden didn't apologize. Nor did he stoop to help me collect the egg carton, which was upended in a gelatinous mess on my hardwood floor. "Mr. Katz would like to know when breakfast will be ready." His eyes bulged behind the thick lenses of his glasses. With his oily pale skin and lanky body, he reminded me of some kind of cave-dwelling amphibian. I wished he'd crawl back into his hole.

I bent down to inventory the carton; only three of the dozen had survived. "Well, now that we're out of eggs, it will be a few minutes later." It occurred to me that I hadn't considered him when doing the breakfast tally. Although Ogden generally stuck to his boss like glue, it was easy to forget he existed. "Are you going to be joining them?"

"Of course. But do try to hurry. Mr. Katz has an extremely busy schedule."

"Well, I'm afraid breakfast will be slightly delayed." I tipped my chin toward the mess on the floor. "But I'll see what I can do."

The oven timer buzzed as Ogden slipped through the swinging door to the dining room. I rescued the cake from the oven and squatted to clean up the mess on the floor. What kind of urgent business could Bernard Katz have on an island of less than a square mile? Most of the movers and shakers here were fishermen's wives after a few too many beers. I hoped Barbara Eggleby would be able to convince the board that the Shoreline Conservation Association was the right choice for the land next door. The Katz development would be a cancer on the island. Lord knew the Katzes were.

I raced up the stairs and knocked on my niece's door. Gwen had come to work with me for the summer, cleaning the rooms, covering the phones, and helping with the cooking from time to time in exchange for room and board. The help was a godsend— not only was it free, but it allowed me time to work on promoting the inn—but Gwen was not a perfect assistant.

Part of the reason Gwen was spending the summer at the inn was that her mother didn't know what else to do with her: she'd flunked half of her classes her first year at UCLA and my sister couldn't spend more than ten minutes in the same room with her daughter without one or the other of them declaring war. Her work at the inn, while not F-level, was between a B and a C, when I needed everything to be A+. Still, help was help, and beggars couldn't be choosers. I wished that some of the enthusiasm she showed for the art classes she was taking on the island would spill over to her housekeeping skills.

"Who is it?" answered a groggy voice from the other side of the door. I cracked the door open. Gwen's hair was a messy brown halo in the dim light from the curtained window.

"I'm sorry to wake you, but I need you to run down to Charlene's and get a dozen eggs."

"What time is it?"

"It's just after seven. Please hurry... I've got guests waiting."

She groaned. "Seven in the *morning*?"

"I know. But it's an emergency." She grumbled something and began to move toward the side of the bed, so I closed the door and jogged back down the stairs. I'd start with fruit salad and a plate of coffee cake, and bring out the eggs later. Maybe a pan of sausage, too... I could keep it warm until the Bittles came down at 8:30.

I was retrieving a package of pork sausages from the freezer when someone tapped on the door to the back porch. I whirled around to tell the Katzes I'd meet them in the dining room shortly, and saw the sun-streaked brown hair of my neighbor, John Quinton. "Come in!" I hollered, smiling for the first time that morning.

John's green eyes twinkled in a face already brown from afternoons out on the water in his sailboat, and his faded green T-shirt and shorts were streaked with sawdust. John was both a friend and a tenant; he rented the inn's converted carriage house from me, as well as a small shed he had converted to a workshop. He was a sculptor who created beautiful things from the driftwood that washed up on the beaches, but supplemented what he called his "art habit" with a variety of part-time jobs. In the spring and summer, he made toy sailboats for the gift shop on the pier. He also held a year-round job as the island's only deputy.

"You're up early. Working on a new project?" I asked.

"Island Artists ordered a few more boats. I figured I'd churn them out this morning and then start on some fun stuff." His eyes glinted with mischief. "One of Claudette's goats was eyeing your sweet peas, by the way. I shooed her off, but I'm afraid she'll be back."

I groaned. Claudette White was one of the three members of *Save Our Terns*, and was known on the island as "eccentric." Although her husband, Eleazer, was a boat-builder and popular with the locals, most of the islanders gave Claudette a wide berth. Her goats were almost as unpopular as she was, since they were notorious for escaping and consuming other people's gardens.

When Claudette wasn't caring for her goats or knitting their wool into sweaters and hats, she was holding forth at length about the evils of the modern world to anyone who would listen. I wasn't delighted that she had chosen to join *Save Our Terns*, but since the only other takers had been my best friend, Charlene, and me, we didn't feel we could turn her down.

John watched me pry sausage links out of a box and into a cast-iron pan. "I'm not the only one up early. I thought breakfast wasn't till 8:30."

"Yeah, well, we're working on Katz time today." A thump came from overhead, and then the sound of the shower. I sighed: so much for urgency. Gwen must be performing her morning ablutions. I appealed to John for help. "Do you have any eggs I can borrow? I was going to send Gwen down to the store, but I'm short on time."

"I just picked up a dozen yesterday. Is that enough?"

"You're a lifesaver." He disappeared through the back door, and the thought flitted through my mind that he might stay for a cup of coffee when he got back. I spooned fruit salad into a crystal bowl and reminded myself that John had a girlfriend in Portland. Five minutes later I sailed into the dining room bearing the fruit salad and a platter mounded with hot coffee cake. Stanley Katz had arrived, and sat hunched in an ill-fitting brown suit next to his wife. Estelle glared at me. “Coffee cake? I can’t eat that. I thought this breakfast was supposed to be low-fat!” Then she pointed a lacquered nail at the ginger-colored cat who had curled up in a sunbeam on the windowsill. “And why is there a *cat* in your dining room? Surely that’s against health department regulations?”

I scooped up Biscuit and deposited her in the living room. She narrowed her gold-green eyes at me and stalked over to the sofa as I hurried back into the dining room. “I’ll have skinny scrambled eggs and wheat toast out shortly,” I said. “We had a slight mishap in the kitchen.” I shot Ogden a look. He blinked behind his thick lenses. I attempted a bright smile. “Can I get anybody more coffee?”

Estelle sighed. “I suppose so.” She turned to her father-in-law, who had already transferred two pieces of cake to his plate. “With this kind of service,” she muttered under her breath, “I don’t know how she expects to stay in business.”

When I got back into the kitchen, a carton of eggs lay on the butcher-block counter. Darn. I’d missed John. The sausages had started to sizzle and Estelle’s egg whites were almost done when the phone rang.

“Nat.”

“Charlene? You’re up early.” Charlene was the local grocer, a fellow member of *Save Our Terns*, and my source for island gossip. She was also my best friend.

“I’ve got bad news.”

I groaned. “You’re kidding. The Katzes sprang a surprise 7 a.m. breakfast on me and then his assistant broke all of my eggs. It can’t get any worse.”

“It can. I just talked to the coastal airport: no planes in or out, probably for the whole day. A big nor’easter is about to hit the coast.”

My heart thumped in my chest. “The airport is closed? So Barbara isn’t going to make it in time for the council meeting?”

“It’s just you and me, babe. And Claudette.”

My stomach sank. Without a representative from the Shoreline Conservation Association to combat Katz’s offer for the property next to the inn, we could only sit and watch as Katz wooed the board of selectmen with visions of the fat bank accounts the island would enjoy when the Cranberry Island Premier Resort came into being.

I leaned my head against the wall. “We’re sunk.”

Download your copy of Murder on the Rocks now to find out what happens next!

Praise for the Gray Whale Inn mysteries...

"This book is an absolute gem." — Suspense Magazine

"Deliciously clever plot. Juicy characters. Karen MacInerney has cooked up a winning recipe for murder. **Don't miss this mystery!**" — *New York Times* Bestselling Author Maggie Sefton

"...a new **cozy author worth investigating.**" — Publishers Weekly

"Murder on the Rocks mixes a pinch of salt air, a hunky love interest, an island divided by environmental issues... and, of course, murder. **Add Karen MacInerney to your list of favorite Maine mystery authors.**" — Lea Wait, author of the Antique Print mystery series

"**Sure to please cozy readers.**" — Library Journal

"I look anxiously forward to the sequel... Karen MacInerney has a **winning recipe for a great series.**" — Julie Obermiller, Features Editor, Mysterical-E

MORE BOOKS BY KAREN MACINERNEY

To download a free book and receive members-only outtakes, giveaways, short stories, recipes, and updates, join Karen's Reader's Circle at www.karenmacinerney.com! You can also join her Facebook community; she often hosts giveaways and loves getting to know her readers there.

And don't forget to follow her on BookBub to get newsflashes on new releases!

The Snug Harbor Mysteries

A Killer Ending

Inked Out

The Lies that Bind

The Gray Whale Inn Mysteries

Murder on the Rocks

Dead and Berried

Murder Most Maine

Berried to the Hilt

Brush With Death
Death Runs Adrift
Whale of a Crime
Claws for Alarm
Scone Cold Dead
Anchored Inn
Basket Case (A Gray Whale Inn Novella)
Cookbook: The Gray Whale Inn Kitchen
Four Seasons of Mystery (A Gray Whale Inn Collection)
Blueberry Blues (A Gray Whale Inn Short Story)
Pumpkin Pied (A Gray Whale Inn Short Story)
Iced Inn (A Gray Whale Inn Short Story)
Lupine Lies (A Gray Whale Inn Short Story)

The Dewberry Farm Mysteries

Killer Jam
Fatal Frost
Deadly Brew
Mistletoe Murder
Dyeing Season
Wicked Harvest
Sweet Revenge
Peach Clobber
Slay Bells Ring: A Dewberry Farm Christmas Story
Cookbook: Lucy's Farmhouse Kitchen

The Margie Peterson Mysteries

Mother's Day Out
Mother Knows Best
Mother's Little Helper

Wolves and the City

Howling at the Moon
On the Prowl
Leader of the Pack

RECIPES

TEXAS TOMATO PIE

INGREDIENTS

- 4 large tomatoes, peeled and sliced
- 9-Inch pie shell deep-dish
- 1 cup mozzarella cheese, grated
- 1 cup cheddar cheese grated
- 1/2 cup sour cream
- 3 tablespoons mayonnaise
- salt and pepper
- 4 basil leaves

Instructions

1. Preheat oven to 350°F and bake pie shell until lightly browned.
2. While oven is heating and pie shell is baking, peel and slice tomatoes, place in a colander and sprinkle with salt. Allow to drain for 10 minutes.

3. Stir together sour cream and mayonnaise, then add cheeses and salt and pepper. Layer tomatoes in pie shell and spread the sour cream mixture on top.
4. Bake 30 minutes until lightly browned and cheese is melted. Remove from oven and sprinkle torn basil leaves on top. Cool slightly and serve warm.

MIGAS

INGREDIENTS

- 12 large eggs
- 1/4 cup milk
- 1/2 teaspoon each ground cumin, fine sea salt, freshly-cracked black pepper
- 1 tablespoon olive oil
- 1 small white onion, peeled and diced
- 1 jalapeño, seeded and finely chopped
- 3 cloves garlic, minced
- 2 large handfuls corn tortilla chips, roughly crumbled
- 2/3 cup salsa, homemade or store-bought
- 2/3 cup shredded Mexican-blend cheese, plus extra for serving
- TOPPINGS:
- Chopped fresh cilantro
- Diced red onion
- Sliced avocado

- Diced tomato
- Extra salsa

INSTRUCTIONS

1. In a large bowl, whisk together eggs, milk, cumin, salt and pepper. Set aside.
2. Heat olive oil over medium-high heat in a large sauté pan. Add onion and jalapeño and sauté, stirring occasionally, until the onion is soft and translucent; add garlic and sauté for 1-2 additional minutes, stirring occasionally, until the garlic is fragrant but not brown.
3. Add the egg mixture and reduce heat to medium. Cook for 5-6 minutes, stirring frequently, until the eggs are completely scrambled.
4. Stir in the tortilla chips, salsa and cheese and cook for 2 minutes, stirring occasionally. Taste and season with extra salt and pepper if needed.
5. Serve warm, garnished with cilantro, onion, avocado, tomato, and extra salsa.

DEWBERRY PIE BARS

INGREDIENTS

CRUST & CRUMBS

- 2 cups all-purpose flour
- 1/4 tsp baking soda
- 1/4 tsp salt
- 1/4 tsp cinnamon
- 3/4 cup unsalted butter, melted
- 1/2 cup granulated sugar
- 1/4 cup light brown sugar
- 1 tsp vanilla extract
- 1 tsp lemon zest

DEWBERRY FILLING

- 2 1/2 cups dewberries (or blackberries), frozen or fresh
- 3/4 cup granulated sugar
- 1/8 tsp salt

- 3 Tbsp cornstarch
- 1 tsp lemon zest
- 1/2 Tbsp lemon juice

INSTRUCTIONS

1. Preheat oven to 350°F and line an 8-inch square baking pan with parchment paper.
2. In a medium bowl, with a fork, whisk together flour, baking soda, salt, and cinnamon. In a separate large bowl, whisk together melted butter, sugar, brown sugar, vanilla, and lemon zest until combined. Add dry ingredients to the butter mixture and fold in with a wooden spoon until incorporated.
3. Set aside 3/4 cup of crust dough for topping and put in refrigerator to chill until ready to use. Press remaining dough evenly into bottom of prepared baking pan.
4. Bake crust for 14 to 16 minutes, until lightly golden and set. Transfer to a wire rack and let cool for 15 minutes.
5. While crust is cooling, combine berries, sugar, salt, cornstarch, lemon zest, and lemon juice in a heavy saucepan over medium-high heat. Bring to a boil, pressing firmly on berries with the back of a spoon to release juices, for about 3 to 4 minutes. Reduce heat to low and simmer for 1 to 2 minutes, or until dewberry filling is thickened and coats the back of a spoon. Remove pan from the heat and cool for 10 minutes.

6. Once filling has cooled, spoon over cooled crust. Crumble chilled, reserved dough over filling.
7. Return pan to oven and bake for another 40 minutes, or until topping is golden and filling slightly bubbly. Cool completely in pan on a wire rack.
8. Just before cutting, chill bars in the freezer for 15 minutes. Once cool, carefully lift parchment and place bars on a cutting board; cut into squares with a sharp knife. Store bars in an airtight container in the refrigerator.

CARNITAS (MEXICAN PULLED PORK)

Ingredients

- 5 pounds pork chunks from various cuts (loin, butt, pork belly, etc... leave bones in if you can and be flexible with the weight... it's what fits into your pot)
- Salt
- 3 quarts lard
- Zest of 3 oranges
- 5 bay leaves
- 1 white onion, quartered
- 1 head garlic, sliced in half
- For serving:
- chopped onion
- cilantro
- salsa
- corn or flour tortillas warmed

Instructions

1. Salt the pork chunks, leaving the bones in if they will fit in your pot.
2. Fill a large pot with the lard and heat it to about 200°F.
3. When the lard hits temperature, add the pork and the remaining ingredients and let things cook at about 195°F, more or less, until pork is soft and tender, or about 4 hours, depending on the cut (loin cooks faster, so if you're using a mix of cuts, add the loin in the last hour or so).
4. When the meat is starting to fall off the bone, remove it from the lard and let it cool a bit. Carefully debone it, if necessary, and heat the lard to 350°F and fry the pork until the exterior is crispy. (If you want to reuse the lard, remove all but about 1 cup and then sear the pork bits in that lard until crispy.)
5. Chop and shred the meat, then serve. I like this on corn tortillas with chopped onion, cilantro, and green salsa... yum!

AGUA DE SANDÍA (WATERMELON WATER)

Ingredients

- 4 pounds watermelon (about 12 cups chunked)
- 8 cups water
- ¼ - ½ cup sugar
- Ice
- Mint sprigs
- Lime wedges

Instructions

1. Cut watermelon into small chunks, removing seeds if necessary, and transfer half of the chunks to a blender.
2. Add 1 cup of water and mix on high until smooth. Transfer juice to a large pitcher and repeat the same process with the other half of the watermelon.

3. Add the rest of the water to the pitcher along with ¼ cup sugar; stir. Add more water or sugar to taste. (I sometimes also add some fresh lime juice to add some zing!)
4. Transfer the jar to the fridge to chill for a few hours, or serve immediately over ice with mint sprigs or lime wedges.

ACKNOWLEDGMENTS

A big shout-out to my mother, Carol Swartz, for being an early reader. Angelika Offenwanger was a terrific editor as always (any mistakes are mine, not hers), and thank you also to my beta readers, particularly Katherine Anderson, Tricia DeVito, Kay Pucciarelli, Julia Hunter, Tanya Jackson, Tina Thomas, Federica De Dominicis, Carla Brauer, Mandy Young Kutz, Sandy Webster, Elizabeth Caldwell, Kelly Nguyen, Tyna Derhay, and Vicky May for their careful reading and great "oops" catches! I am ever grateful, as always, to the amazing Kim Killion for her beautiful cover design.

And from the bottom of my heart, thank you to my amazing Facebook community and the members of my Readers' Circle for your inspiration, encouragement, and support. Writing can be a lonely business, but you make me feel like you're right there with me. It takes a village to write a mystery, and I couldn't do it without you!

ABOUT THE AUTHOR

Karen is the housework-impaired, award-winning author of multiple mystery series, and her victims number well into the double digits. She lives in Austin, Texas with her sassy family, Tristan, and Little Bit (a.k.a. Dog #1 and Dog #2).

Feel free to visit Karen's web site, where you can download a free book and sign up for her Readers' Circle to receive subscriber-only short stories, deleted scenes, recipes and other bonus material. You can also find her on Facebook (she spends an inordinate amount of time there), where Karen loves getting to know her readers, answering questions, and offering quirky, behind-the-scenes looks at the writing process (and life in general). And please follow her on Bookbub to find out about new releases and sales!

P. S. Don't forget to follow Karen on BookBub to get newsflashes on new releases!

www.karenmacinerney.com
karen@karenmacinerney.com

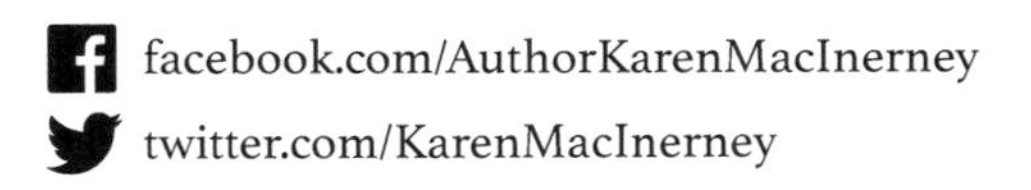

Printed in Great Britain
by Amazon